Yours, and Mine

Yours, and Mine

Novella and Stories

by Judith Rascoe

AN ATLANTIC MONTHLY PRESS BOOK
Little, Brown and Company — Boston—Toronto

FIRST EDITION

T 05/73

Library of Congress Cataloging in Publication Data

Rascoe, Judith.
    Yours, and mine.

    "An Atlantic Monthly Press book"
    I. Title.
PZ4.R222Yo [PS3568.A65]   813'.5'4   72-12595
ISBN 0-316-75634-2

ATLANTIC–LITTLE, BROWN BOOKS
ARE PUBLISHED BY
LITTLE, BROWN AND COMPANY
IN ASSOCIATION WITH
THE ATLANTIC MONTHLY PRESS

*Published simultaneously in Canada
by Little, Brown & Company (Canada) Limited*

PRINTED IN THE UNITED STATES OF AMERICA

For Clancy and Roger

Contents

Part One

Yours, and Mine

One

An old woman named Leona wrote to me from Santa Barbara on her mournful green stationery —

> We're all very sad about the oil. It would make you cry
> to see the lovely beaches all ruined.

Would it? There was a public beach in San Francisco where my mother took me when I was seven or eight, and I remember her voice: "Don't get in the oil." I lifted my foot and saw a rich brown smear on my instep. I remember also the marbled sky and the rotten, salty smell of the water. Of all places I liked the beach best. Oil, then, was part of the beach — I found clamshells, crabs' legs, kelp and oil: on the stones, in the sand, and on lengths of rope.

Years later, on another beach, somebody said: "Don't swim, you'll get oil on your suit." I saw far away the sun standing over a great bank of cloud that ran the length of the horizon. It might have been the coast of China. The cold golden sea swelled and foamed and fell deafeningly. That was how night sounded, like the surf growing louder. Confused, I ran into the water. When I came back somebody said: "Did you get oil on your suit?" It was too dark to see.

Two

I live in New York now, and one night in June last year I was riding home on the bus. A woman with a little baby sat across from me, and an old black woman sat beside me,

3

squirming and bobbing her disordered head. She began to sing a ragtime song. The baby laughed and shrieked and wriggled to get out of its mother's arms. Somebody said, "The baby's tired, poor thing." The black woman stopped singing. "Baby ain't got no right to everything," she said. "I got the right to ride this bus. This bus for people like me. Everybody pay attention to the baby, nothin' very special about a baby. A baby ain't worth nothin'. Why everybody makin' such a fuss over a baby, I don't know." She started to sing her rag-time song again — she had a strong, true voice — and the baby's mother looked around for somebody to smile at, to show that she didn't mind, that she wasn't afraid of the poor old woman.

I jumped off the bus and ran home and sat by the window for a while, looking at the lights. Tell me something, I was thinking. Tell me something. Then the telephone rang. It was Leona, calling from Santa Barbara: Happy Birthday.

"I saw John Butler at the museum the other night," she said. "He said you were having a good time in New York."

"Oh, yes."

"I guess you don't have any plans to come out here," she said.

"No," I said. "I'm coming next week. I'll take a plane to San Jose and see my parents and then I'll take a train down to see you."

"All that way," she said, trying it on for size.

"It's easy," I said.

A few minutes after she hung up, somebody else remembered it was my birthday and called to invite me to a party. He wanted to talk to his lawyer about his divorce, and so I spent most of the evening sitting next to a long, thin rich girl who had learned that she didn't have to smile or take an interest in other people: she was very beautiful as well as rich.

She told me about her dermatologist. After a while her boy-friend came over and tried to get her started again by telling her I was a film editor. "I'm into film," she said. Oh, yes? A friend of hers made a movie in Dubrovnik last year and she played a peasant girl, and then later in Paris he introduced her to Alain Delon who turned out to be a friend of a girl she'd gone to school with, and he said she should study acting but then they all went to Gstaad instead, but she really wanted to direct. "That's great," I said. Under other circumstances I would have wanted to hit her, but now I didn't mind, because I was going to Santa Barbara. I didn't tell anybody I was going, but that's all I thought about for the next three days — amazed that it was so simple; it wouldn't take years and years to go back to Santa Barbara. It only had taken years and years to leave it.

Three

In San Jose I sat in the backyard of my parents' house, eating Mexican TV dinners. My mother's flowers in the six o'clock light looked as if they'd been painted with Day-Glo. The air smelled of cars. She asked me if I knew this man and that man in the motion picture business, but they were all dead and squashed beneath the weight of their mausoleums. My father said that New York was full of Jews, but he didn't mind — they'd keep me on my toes. He liked New York: there were a lot of doggone swell little places to eat that his friend Earl Fahd used to take him to that summer he was there, fifteen years ago. After dinner my mother took me downstairs to the "recreation room" and showed me her albums from the days when she had been a bit player: there were dozens of stills where she stood, smiling with deep concentration, behind the featured players. "We had lots of fun," she said. She began to cry. My father had suggested a separation. When I was five they'd started their divorce; when I was in college they'd remarried, grimly. I thought they'd run out of hope, but now my mother was weeping because she thought he had a girlfriend. She lifted her face to me as if to a camera: where would she find somebody else? the look said. I asked her, "What do you want to do?" She wanted him to take her to Hawaii.

After she went to bed my father and I played pinochle and talked about the real estate business because he was a salesman for Loebbler Realty. Part time, something to do. He liked the big schemes and the big deals, but he shook his head over them: the boom can't last. Another slump was coming and another boom after that — he has a farmer's long view for time, despite everything.

"I used to be ambitious," he told me. "I thought I was going to set the world on fire." But he was nervous and merry. He wouldn't talk about leaving my mother, but he had the air of a man who's packed his bags.

The next morning I went with him down to Loebbler Realty, a grimy little Spanish hacienda between an auto supply store and a laundromat. Ken Loebbler had gotten old and so had Myrna, the secretary, and everything in the office was out of date now, but Ken was planning to sell the place, open a new office in a new shopping mall on the edge of the city. They were all going to start fresh again. "I got your Dad talked into working full time," Ken said. I wanted to shake my father's hand and say: Congratulations on your New Life. "We'll see," my father said. "We'll see how it goes."

He couldn't understand why I wanted to take the train to Santa Barbara when the plane was so cheap and fast; but he remembered it used to be a swell train — he remembered the

Lark and long dining cars and fresh linen and lambchops for breakfast. Oh, well, I said, buying sandwiches at the station.

Four

When I got on the train I had pencils and notepads and envelopes, because I thought I could put my life in order; but instead I rocked dozily, hour after hour, watching the landscape drift and change as slowly as a cloud: orchards first, and then the misty coastal plain off Santa Cruz, and the long Salinas Valley. The railroad follows the Camino Real, winding among the mission churches, a litany of saints: Santa Clara, San Jose, San Carlos Borromeo, San Juan Bautista, Nuestra Señora de la Soledad. San Antonio, San Miguel, San Luis Obispo. Protect us. The valley is the landscape of dreams where we fly like doves and find the dead waiting with smiles. In the parallax of vision the hills turn sinuously: plump Ingres nudes, corpse-tinted, their pink earth blued by distance. I saw hawks and cows. The train rose up into a mountain pass, then rushed to the sea's edge: all multiplicity, all simple things turned to one great blue vastness. Up and down the train faces turned toward the windows to stare — is this what we've come for?

Five

In Santa Barbara, in the late afternoon, the train arrived amidst the festivity of crossing bells. I got off, the train went on, the silence fell to the drumming of pigeons in the station eaves. A boy with a knapsack lay asleep under an oleander

7

across the tracks. Leona was sitting in the Ladies Waiting Room, as still as a shaft of light. "I thought they'd torn this place down," she said when she stood up to greet me. We went out to her big white Lincoln, and she drove very slowly along the beach highway, letting the little cars slip around her as they would. Then she turned up into the hills toward her house.

"It hasn't changed much," I said.

"Oh, yes, it has," she said.

At her doorstep Leona plants jasmine. I lifted a branch to my nose.

"Welcome back," Leona said. "Mrs. Gomez isn't here this afternoon, we'll have to do for ourselves."

In the kitchen I opened a dish cupboard and met the fragrance of my grandmother's cupboards: a California odor — the clean mustiness of wood grown old. I looked at Leona's back. If I told her about the smell of the cupboard she would frown and say, "I don't think my cupboards *smell*."

She always had the same advice for me: "What's done's done. No sense crying over old times. Some day I'm going to sell this house and get rid of all this old trash." Every winter she rented a house in Palm Springs with Mrs. Galleon. They also went to Acapulco, and once she'd sent me a purse, woven from pale blond fiber and sewn with pearls, rhinestones and colored yarn. I liked it but it puzzled me — where did she think I might carry such a purse? A week later there came a note: she and Mrs. Galleon were studying Yoga.

We took our tea back into the living room.

"There's no reason on earth for you to come back here," Leona said, in preparation for a nice long gossip about what had been going on in Santa Barbara. She regarded me sentimentally, but the sentiment cost her more now because she was past seventy, her children were dead, and her heavy diamond rings, set in white gold, were wrapped with bits of adhesive tape to keep them on her shrinking fingers. All about her she saw decay: "You can't get anything decent in those stores downtown, just cheap flashy stuff . . . nobody gardens like we used to — how can we? all the good Japs have died . . . I went into the hotel and I just about cried. All those big creepers had fallen down into the patio. . . . Cabby Butler's got himself a golf car now, so I guess he'll die in harness . . . John was staying with him for a while, but now . . ." And she shut her mouth quickly.

"But now?"

She coughed.

"I always thought that you and John were a pair," she said.

"I thought so too," I said.

"But he came back here all by himself." She gave me a look, as if to say: That's that, done's done. Everything ends: that's what *she* knew.

"I'm going to see him," I said.

"I suppose so." She was silent for a moment, and then she made an impatient gesture with her head: this was her house, after all. She picked up my empty cup and set it on the tray. She was waiting for me to say something, and when I didn't, she burst out at last, "You can't always have your own way."

"No," I said.

"Now don't get gloomy." And then, with a little flick of jealousy, "I guess you came to see him."

"No, I came to see you."

It was true, but how could she believe it?

"Well I guess you have to do that while you can," she said. "I'm bound to go any day now." She stood up and gave me a kiss on the cheek. "I'm awful glad to see you, honey. You stay here as long as you like." But a little later she gave me a queer, assaying look, as if she knew me better than I knew myself — which she probably did. I almost said to her: Leona, tell me my fortune. But I was afraid to.

That night after she went to bed I took a walk through the house. Built in the twenties, in the Andalusian style with red tile roofs and white plaster walls and tiled floors, it was famous for awhile — but seldom loved, I think. The walls rise too far and the rooms are too big, and all the luxuries that money have poured into it have not appeased it — rather, the things take sides with the house against the shortcomings of its inhabitants. The storks and iris in the Chinese pewter basins are content with the operatic shadows of the staircase; the Chinese carpets translate the natural disorder of the gardens into ritual shapes. From time to time Leona threatens to sell it and scatter its contents at auction, but I've never believed she will really do this. Her threat is a way for her to say: This is mine, I am not possessed by this house but its owner. How else could she say it? She's frail and moves slowly, but with determination, to cross the wide rooms toward the sunlight. But when I walk through the house I have a game of my own: catch me if you can.

Six

At breakfast Leona said, "Your brother called me."

Suddenly I was so attentive that I forgot I'd scarcely been listening.

"I don't believe it!" I said.

Leona frowned. "I don't see why you'd think I'd lie about it."

"I mean I'm surprised."

"I was surprised too," she said indignantly. "I told him, *Eddie,* I said, *I don't know why you're calling me.*" She glanced away, embarrassed. Then she looked at me again. "I gave him your address. Well, he should know you and I are in touch. There's nothing wrong with that." Another swerve of her eyes, as if she wondered if there might not be after all something wrong with that.

"Is there something wrong with that?" I asked.

"I don't like people picking my brains to know what I know." Her lips moved silently, then: "I'd have been happy to have him come here any time he wanted to come. He was a beautiful little boy. Years ago I sent him a note and I never got any reply. I naturally took an interest in him because your grandmother was my friend.

"But I know how your people carried on! I said a long time ago, a friend is one thing but I can't get mixed up in a family quarrel. You're nobody's friend if you do that and I'm sure your grandmother would have agreed with me about that."

"Did you tell him I was coming?"

"No, I didn't know about that."

A miserable silence followed.

There I sat, drinking her coffee, scattering crumbs on her table, dirtying her ashtray, scuffing the rug. And I was about to go upstairs again to soil her towels, wrinkle her sheets, smoke up the bedroom and get lipstick on the water glasses. What good had all that money done her if she had to put up with the likes of me? and my brother.

"I'll go to see him when I'm in San Francisco," I said.

Her thoughts were busy elsewhere. She told me where: "Don't you ever write to him?"

"I'm no good at writing letters. And it's been many years — I'm scared to."

"That's silly," she said, but she had relented. "Not that there's any reason on this earth why you should keep in touch with him. And there is something peculiar about him. He's here in Santa Barbara."

I must have looked around the room: I couldn't remember if Leona liked awful surprises. But the house was so still that I could hear an electric clock wheezing in the kitchen. Leona went on to explain that he had called her from a motel (she couldn't remember its name) saying he'd be in town for about a week and would get in touch with her again. "For a 'drink' he said, and I didn't like the way he said it."

"I'll talk to him," I said.

"There's no reason I shouldn't talk to him, is there?" She was genuinely bewildered, and characteristically she expressed this by getting angry. I assured her — with the frozen gaze of the liar — that there was no reason at all. She might even like Eddie. For that matter, so might I. I hadn't seen him since I was six years old.

Seven

There was a rapping on the glass, like the sound of a branch: Mr. Takeda, the gardener, stood outside the French doors with a tank of spray strapped to his back. Leona jumped up to talk to him and they went off together into the garden looking for monsters and disease; I stayed behind because I didn't want to hear their conversation — listening to the two of them, one begins to see the garden as a hospital ward full of bad cases: infestations of fungus and parasites. Atrophied limbs. Cancer. Love is pain: children die, dogs get run over, trees wither. I thought: she knows better than I. Then old habit caught me. I went up to my room to call John, and as I passed through the house I thought: *familiar-*

ity is like a drug, and at that instant its trance deserted me and I was full of dread.

When I was in New York, and John was far away, I thought I knew how to love him: the quarrel between us dwindled to the little tariffs one pays when one crosses into another's privacy. And he'd paid too: when we lived together in New York he had to put up with my stubbornness and my sulks, my unwashed kitchen floor, the ugly things I said about Chinese cooking and the way I fell asleep at expensive concerts. And worse. But didn't we boast about the price we paid for living together? to say to our friends: We aren't just any couple! We thought they believed us.

But near him again now, I felt it: a senseless alarm, the sort one feels waking in the middle of the night, roused by a sound no longer audible, a movement perceived in sleep and stilled on awakening. I believed the cause of it must be obvious to everyone but me: when he left New York I was surprised to learn that nobody was surprised by our separation. I'd insisted: *We're more alike than you think.*

"What are you going to do in Santa Barbara?" I asked him while he was packing.

"I'm going to study hawks," he said.

"Where?"

"In the valleys."

"Are you going to teach?"

"No."

When he finished we went out for supper and I saw that he didn't look at anything, that his body bent against the surrounding city, as if nothing there were of any interest to him now. In the café he wouldn't look at another person — or at me; he just sat eating his sandwich very slowly and talking about the kind of camera he wanted to buy to photograph hawks. And I sat there *drawing him out,* as I might pull conversation from a stranger. Then we went home and that was our last night together. "I'm not going with you. I'll never go back to that fucking town," I said. "Nobody's asking you," he said.

I called his uncle, Cabby Butler, to get John's number; but John answered the phone. I'm here, I said. "I'd like to see you," he said. And so he appeared ten minutes later, driving his uncle's plum-colored Mercedes and wearing an embroidered Mexican shirt.

"Oh, John, your hair is beautiful!" And so it was, long and blond.

"You look tired," he said.

I took off my shoes and curled up on the leather seat and John drove the plum-colored Mercedes up and down the hillsides of Santa Barbara.

"Tell me what you've been doing," I said.

He laughed out loud. "You want to have an opinion about me," he said. "You want to compare yourself."

"Yes," I said, delighted to be surprised, again, at last. "I don't want to compare myself with anyone else."

"Oh, is that what you've learned in the meantime?"

"Well, it's a principle," I said. "I ought to have something to aim for. It's almost too hard for me — that's why I've adopted it."

He shook his head.

"You do as you like," I insisted.

"Everybody does that," he said. "Most people make themselves unhappy by telling themselves they want to be doing something else."

"Bullshit."

"Absolutely," he said, very cheerfully.

"Ah, but it's the best I can do, isn't it?" Lying, thinking: *I want something else too.* What?

"Maybe."

"Thank you for the doubt," I said.

Eight

The plum-colored Mercedes moved slowly and throbbingly along the narrow streets, and leaves splashed against the windows, dust and the smell of eucalyptus blew into the car. Now and then we passed a garden that burgeoned in the marine shadow of a live oak, a garden without flowers but full of thrusting leaves. The car turned, the sun fell directly through the windshield, scorching my face, so that I closed my eyes for a moment and opened them again to find all the colors changed to electric, bluish hues, as if I had been asleep. Perhaps I had been asleep. For although I stared at the houses and the gardens, after a time I couldn't see any more of them. They no longer distinguished themselves, they no longer excited me with envy, and I could no longer cast my imagined self down the gravelled drives to the door, through the door and upstairs to a balconied window from which "I" leaned out to watch a plum-colored Mercedes, the bloom of dust still on it, move slowly down the street to disappear in a flash of sunlight where the hill swelled out of the shadow of the oak trees.

Nine

By no accident John and I had known each other since childhood: we both had grandmothers who lived in Santa

Barbara. Now it is a peculiar fact about the town, and about others like it in California, that it is a place where grandmothers live and receive the spouses and offspring of their children's and their grandchildren's many marriages. The old wives and the new wives and the brides-to-be, the old husbands and new husbands and boyfriends all sweep through the house like nomadic tribesmen, bearing their children-by-a-former-marriage, their trunks full of community property, their hair-dryers, electro-massagers, sunlamps, travel-irons, humidifiers, and transistor radios. They leave behind cocktail dresses with cigarette burns in the skirt, broken brassieres, undershirts, stained neckties, bottle warmers and stacks of *Sports Illustrated;* and they make off with what they choose to call heirlooms and most of the washcloths. At Christmastime there is a snowstorm of cards. The grandmother opens the envelope with the letter-opener that Helen's first husband gave her and finds a colored photograph of Helen's second husband and his new wife, Myrna, surrounded by Myrna's children from her first marriage: "Season's Greetings from the Hannibals!"

One woman I used to know had gone through this with three children — nine marriages, five grandchildren, eleven lateral grandchildren (the language has no word yet to describe these offspring of former husbands by former wives, et cetera). She asked me once how I could expect her to love them all. But she did love them all, I think, even though she seemed to give each one a civil service rating, as it were, that depended on degree of kinship, moral character, and time spent on the job. Every Christmas she sent out Mission-Pak fruit assortments: those with high ratings received apricots in brandy, while the lower ranks had to be content with dates and dried prunes.

John and I were members of such families, and during our

childhood we had often taken shelter with our Santa Barbara grandmothers. This sheltering was a bewildering thing. It occurred when our fathers and mothers started raising their voices at each other; as the marriages waned we spent more and more time with our grandmothers, in a condition of serenity and security that we had never known at home, and I wonder if we did not come to believe that divorce was a state of being, a euphoria, a relief.

I know that John told me that when he broke his first engagement and fled, after graduation from Berkeley and the vibrant silence of the marriage announcement that didn't occur, to his grandmother's house, he felt, he said, very happy — "Like getting in a hot bath and it's too hot and you stay there, anyway, getting groggy and stupid." He made me remember the silent, smothering afternoons when I lay on the wicker divan in my grandmother Kellin's sunporch, far away from all voices, angry and pleasing alike, and felt myself grow transparent, no longer able to distinguish what I saw (a cream-colored window frame, venetian blinds, thin slats of blue sky) from what I imagined as appearing behind me (a cream-colored wall and a panel of brown silk embroidered with a white stork). I could hear a porcelain clock tapping round and round the fractions of seconds; motes of dust rose in a beam of light. I could stand it only so long, and then I'd run into the kitchen, screaming for my grandmother because I was afraid she too had left me alone.

But as I grew older, I realized dimly that in fact I relished these moments of stillness. John did too. And so it has been only with John that I could bear to talk about mysticism or meditation: we could not believe that those people who come from close, noisy, lasting families and got excited about Zen or Yoga could know, as we had, the particular mixture of terror and repose that accompanies such moments, when the self disappears like a mirage from a desert.

But in trying to explain the essential nature of these visits to grandmother, I leave out what is of interest to others: the dramatic marriages.

Mrs. Butler, John's grandmother (after a fashion), had one son, Evan, who was married three times: first to John's mother (a war widow from Lynn, Massachusetts — John's father having perished in the Philippines), and then in turn to a labor organizer and a Swiss practical nurse. The latter wives carried Evan Butler away from Santa Barbara, and John's mother remained the old lady's favorite; when Evan died in Grenoble, the labor organizer and the nurse both re-married quickly and had a couple of uninteresting children, but when they turned up in Santa Barbara, John's mother was already in possession of the fortress, so to speak, and did not relinquish it until John was fourteen and away at school, when she slowly married a retired general. Mrs. Butler died and left the house to her much younger brother, Cabby, and poor Cabby was so used to seeing John in the house that he never seemed to question his right to be there. "It's your home," Cabby often said to John in a puzzled way, and things worked out better than you might expect because John was a gentle and generous boy, a naturalist by pre-occupation, and he spent a lot of time thinking up treats for Cabby like engraved golf tees and Jacuzzi baths; he was, after all, indebted to Cabby for not being made to spend his summers with the retired general.

My own family's ways had been less amiable, and in fact I no longer had any clear reason to come back to Santa Barbara, because my grandmother died years ago — when I was twelve, to be exact — and her house was sold. She and her husband had come into a lot of money very quickly — oil was found on their farm in Louisiana; but it was not soon enough, for she had left a mean, genteel southern family to marry a restless poor man, and her children had all grown up frightened by their poverty. Suddenly the money came and her husband was happy for a few years and then died — in Santa Barbara, where the money had carried them. Her youngest son, Jimmy, my father, married twice, and his wives bore one child apiece: my brother, Eddie, and me.

My father's wives were very alike: both small, epicene actresses, who evidently liked to be photographed standing on the running boards of automobiles or wading, wearing tank suits, in mountain rivers. It was like my father to have failed, disastrously, with one marriage and then march off stubbornly to repeat his mistake with another woman. My mother, Suky, told me that she realized her marriage wouldn't work when she saw an old picture of Estelle wading in the Russian River: Jimmy had taken a picture of Suky similar to it only the week before. They broke up for the first time when I was five, and during the years of separations and reconciliations I spent most of the summers with Grandmother Kellin, Jimmy's mother, in Santa Barbara.

On those summer weekends, when stray members of the family were shoved together in the house like log jams, I hid in the basement and went out only under the escort of the gardener, who dropped by on Saturdays to deal with the snails. Stooping behind the breastworks of hydrangea, I would watch the windows of the house where now and then puzzled faces appeared, as if to call me inside. But they never did — it was the general opinion that these weekends were not suitable to a childish audience. When I returned for dinner, everyone had settled down to a suitable topic like my grandmother's fear of being given Negro blood when she had her gallstone operation.

"Mama, that's nonsense!" they would cry in chorus. "I'm sure that wouldn't happen! Of course they keep it separate!" Over turkey they were united in their suspicion of California ways: somehow a drop of Nigra blood might find its way into their veins. At first I was eager for this to happen, since I took up the notion that they would all turn from pale, pink-nosed folks to handsome coffee colors.

It may be a tribute to the democracy of California that my family and the Butlers (Butler Steel) and Leona (Haggen-burger Construction) got on in some fashion or other, for I am sure that neither the Butlers nor Leona had any special respect for Baptist principles and a cracker terror of Negroes; but I do recall that Mrs. Butler and Leona both spent a lot of time praising my family's manners. Doubtless they had never seen anything so cautious, so nervous and punctilious in their lives as the way the Kellins promptly returned invitations, sent notes, reciprocated gifts pound for pound, and wore three-piece suits for drinks on Sunday. It was impossible to get a Kellin to stay a moment longer than the invitation speci-fied, to take an extra drink or the last cigarette or borrow a magazine or use the telephone. "Your grandfather was some-thing different," Leona once told me, and I was happy to hear it.

In a way, he took the family with him when he went in 1929. After giving each child (two sisters, two brothers) a sum of cash — which each of them squirreled away in stocks so conservative they apparently paid dividends in silver coins, taped to a postcard — my grandfather invested his share in second mortgages, rental properties that attracted bootleggers as tenants, cotton futures, mines and railroads (but not before getting solid value in cruises, cocktail parties, oak furniture and poker games). The Depression turned all that misused money to dust, but my grandfather had died a happy man.

My grandmother, whose share had been invested by her poor-mouth children, lived for another quarter century. Nobody else but my feckless grandfather had ever enjoyed those surprising dollars. Through prosperity and decline my grandmother and her children always believed themselves to be on the edge of beggary (this belief perhaps the principle that bound them to their neighbors in Santa Barbara), the victims of a thieving government, financial sharpers from the East, and their own generous natures.

"I charged Enola less interest than any bank would," my father said once, after a loan to his sister, and showed me the account book.

There was a year or so of dogfighting after my grandfather's death (I discovered the collected letters on this matter), but the heirs soon convinced each other that the wells had indeed gone dry and all the money, aside from the portion that would sustain their mother, had vanished; it was with something like nostalgia that every few years they joined battle over a luncheonette in Summerland (now an unmarked spot under a freeway), the troublesome last remnant of my grandfather's investments. Boom or slump, that patch of land depreciated in value, was rented by a string of luckless veterans, and ate up taxes like popcorn. By the time they could finally agree to divide the tiny return from its sale, my grandmother's house had been reinvested in nursing home fees, and her children were no longer rich by any standard whatsoever. She died unobtrusively, probably relieved to be excused from the humiliations of extreme old age; and her children were probably relieved to bury her, for they could forget that the money had ever existed and return to the homely discontent of the lower middle class.

"I saw your grandmother's friend, Leona Haggenburger, recently," my father wrote to me a few years ago. "But I hon-

estly cannot say I feel easy with her. She's a very proper elderly lady and we don't have much to say to each other. I
doubt whether I'll be visiting her again in the near future."

Ten

I said, "John, I don't know why I'm visiting Leona."

"Wait and find out."

"I will! But if I don't find out, will you tell me? I always
believe you know what I really want to do."

"No," he said. He gave me a smile when I looked for it.
"Why do you worry about it?"

The plum-colored Mercedes was moving up a narrow dirt
road, and through an alley of trees we saw a gold meadow
burning in the sun. On one side of the road the trees gave
way to a cactus hedge. The needles hissed along the side of
the car. I have lived most of my life in places where there are
cactus, but I have never wanted to have any in my house —
not even here in the East, where sometimes I long for the
desert — because they seem to me not exotic but all too familiar. They are what all plants must be at the core. They get
hideously scarred and go on living, unable to cast off the
scarred portions, growing slowly and stubbornly, looking as if
they have the right by their very ugliness to dispute every
inch of ground with man and animal. Oh, I should like to
remember the exact color of the meadow covered with tall
grass, but I remember the cactus more clearly. Perhaps because John stopped the car and we got out and looked at the
mountains and the sea.

Eleven

Sitting on the patio in the late afternoon, sipping her drink, Leona would now and then lift her head and the white wall of the garden would flash as a reflection across her green spectacles, giving her the uncomprehending look of an exile. Like many others among the grandmothers she was not a very social lady. During the springtime of their children's first marriages they had given dinner parties and bridge parties and country club dances for their new children-in-law, but these occasions inevitably became the scenes recalled in the divorce courts: mental cruelty, with witnesses. Then the grandmothers saw only one or two old friends at a time, stayed away from the bridge clubs and country clubs, and fancied Acapulco or Hawaii where others like themselves could be found.

"How are your mother and daddy, dear?"

"Very well," I said, and then because she looked disappointed, I told her about the hints of divorce, my father's new job. My parents would have hated it — to have the mean difficulties of their lives retailed; but I knew, as apparently they did not, that Leona simply had no comprehension of the financial gulf which separated her from them now. She only knew that they, like her, were worried about the cost of continuing their medical insurance. "It would ruin me to get sick," she said placidly. "They take you for everything you've got."

The telephone rang.

Mrs. Gomez brought the telephone outside to Leona, who lifted the receiver. After a little bit she covered it with her hand and pushed up her spectacles to look at me. *It's Eddie,* her lips said, making no sound. I shook my head and then I fled upstairs. Some minutes later Leona came up and sat on the bed beside me.

"Eddie wants to talk to me about your grandmother," she said. "I told him I was expecting you. He said he wanted to 'meet' you."

She went to my suitcase and began absent-mindedly to unpack my clothes.

"Why shouldn't he meet you here?" she asked, and then added that she thought young women were lucky nowadays, since they could buy clothes cheaply and throw them away when they got bored with them. "Do you have a special beau in New York, dear?"

I said, "It'll be awkward. I haven't seen Eddie since I was six."

"I'm sure he's very nice," she said uncertainly. "But his mother was hard to get along with, I always thought. And she had him all that time . . ."

Her lips made a small tuck.

"She was *contrary*," she said, and emptied my ashtray. "I told him to come up here tomorrow afternoon and see me. You'll still be here, won't you?"

"I promise." I held her hand a moment.

"Your hand is so cold!" she said.

"John wants to take us both to dinner tonight," I said.

"That's very nice of him," Leona said, and she left the room smiling.

Twelve

I got out of the bathtub and cranked open the window and it was cold outside and blue. There were fanciful silhouettes

24

of jacaranda, rooftops and chimneys, for all the houses of the district were thrown up in the twenties in pursuit of a vision of Spanish baroque that reached its apotheosis in movie houses where it was liberated from the economies of the *nouveau riche.* Here it is largely ornament and facade: in the daylight you can go around a corner and meet the utilitarian backsides of such houses — sensible doors and windows, and wires that emerge from the stucco like feeding tubes from a geriatric patient. But at dusk you notice the rooftops, bright yellow windows are pricked out of the darkness; and you can see this is how the houses and their gardens were supposed to look. My grandmother kept several old copies of *Everybody's* magazine, and in between the gowns for tea-dancing were drawings of these same blue dusks and filigreed skylines. The Dusenbergs motored through the blue dust, the blue dusk, through the orange groves to Santa Barbara, and motion picture actresses emerged in clouds of fur.

On such an evening Estelle, Eddie's mother, must have emerged from my father's Packard in a cloud of fur, and passed, smiling, among the Baptist lions. She and two sisters had shared a flat in Los Angeles while they worked as extras; but I can tell by her photographs that she had no great success, because on her flapper's body God had set an uncompromising Texas head — all bones and chin. Yet she was the one who married an "oil man" from Santa Barbara, and in a later snapshot she wore a different fur while she held Eddie on her lap. Then came snapshots of Eddie alone in front of my grandmother's birdbath: Estelle had left him and my father and had run back to her sisters in Los Angeles, who in turn had carried her off to Tijuana for a Mexican divorce. She remarried a couple of times and Eddie has step-sisters, but I know nothing about them — as I know nothing about Estelle except the refrain, "She was contrary" (my own mother was, by contrast, "impossible to understand," not, I inferred, the same thing as contrary). Eddie is about fifteen years older than I am, and when I last saw him, in 1947, he had white skin, like everybody else in the family, and beautiful features (not like) and a peculiar sense of humor which I remember only as a sensation, without words. I cannot hear his voice or remember what he said . . .

My grandmother and my mother and my father were there and they all said, "Your brother is coming!" Somebody said he drove a Crosley. I went out on the front steps and began yelling, "A Crosley! A Crosley!" when the car appeared. I knew Eddie would have a car different from anyone else's — a little, dangerous car (according to my father, who had given him a sensible Plymouth, which he'd wrecked) and one he drove recklessly. He sprayed gravel on the hydrangeas and jumped out, and to my delight he also dressed differently from everybody else: he was wearing a zoot suit (according to my father) and a white satin necktie. He hugged me and let me tug at his blond hair, swing his key chain and take off his watch. He brought me a book of nursery rhymes, and when I asked him to read them to me, he changed the words:

> *Little Miss Re-bop-a-dee*
> *Sat on a re-baba-dee-ba*
> *Eating her curds and . . .*
> *Bop-bop-a-roonie!*

After a while, of course, he had to go talk to the grown-ups; my father had been wanting to get a number of things off his chest about Eddie's behavior, education, manner of dress and driving skills. I kept saying, "Eddie, Eddie, read me another nursery rhyme!" — I knew that if my father got everything off his chest Eddie would not come back. I was right.

Eddie did not come back.

But at the time I was used to losing people I liked because of family quarrels; aunts and cousins and even my parents disappeared for months at a time. John and I used to play a game where we named John's soldiers after the people in our families who had disappeared, and fought battles with them on the interesting geography around my grandmother's rock garden.

Not only did Eddie never come back, he even managed to keep anybody from going after him. He went to work as a draftsman in Oakland, and every few years he wrote long, unhappy letters to my father which my father never let me read. I knew only that he had escaped the draft because he had a rheumatic heart and that, as far as anybody knew, he never married.

When I first came to the east coast I felt both liberated from my family and lonely for them. I wrote to my parents and my aunts and uncles and cousins, and finally one night I sat down and wrote a letter to Eddie. Two months later he answered it:

> Well it is good to hear from my only sister. I wish you would send me a photograph of yourself because I don't know what you look like now. I am enclosing a photograph that must look like beautiful you and some pictures of the amazing Bay Area. I work for one of the biggest companies in America and it should get bigger unless the government does what it is trying to do to kill private enterprise in Our Dear Country. Must run now.

The photograph was a newspaper clipping of a pretty girl who looked like Marilyn Monroe. It disturbed me, and I wrote another letter, begging for news of him — what he read, what kind of music he liked, what his job was exactly, and what he remembered about our grandfather. He replied with another letter like the first, answering none of my questions except to say that he had liked our grandfather very much. He added that he was moving; I should write to him at a box number in Sacramento. I thought I would look for his number when I was in San Francisco, but there was never time, during those flying visits to San Jose. Several years later I discovered that the girl in the clipping had been a debutante in Hillsborough.

Once my father came to New York to visit me, and over lunch at the museum we got to talking about Eddie.

"I can't understand him," my father said. "He's got this bee in his bonnet about our having a lot of money and that I should've paid his way through college and given him a lot of trips and that kind of thing. Well, doggone it, I offered to pay his way through college, and he turned me down then, he wouldn't listen to me, and now he's awful bitter about it. He's a grown man now!" He was outraged because Eddie was not being fair, and fairness, I know, has always been the Kellins' implacable virtue.

Thirteen

The blue hour of night passed. When I heard the Mercedes drive up, I went downstairs. John said we were going to eat Mexican food. There was a strong wind and we had to roll up the windows so that Leona could ask John about Cabby's health. I chose to sit in the back seat, and after a while the winding roads made me queasy. I shut my eyes against the sudden lights of oncoming cars and braced myself against the cushions. They asked me if I was all right and I said, *I don't like to drive at night,* and left them to resume their conversation. But I liked this uncomfortable privacy, for not only the car but the sound of the car and the darkness outside isolated me from my "life" (that thing which was to be organized, defined and changed). No one in New York knew where I was now, or why I was here.

Fourteen

My grandmother had a photograph of her mother and her brothers and sisters. It must have been taken on a meager spring day in northern Louisiana: a shadowless pale light falls on the house and the yard and the trees barely in leaf. Two porches span the length of the house, and on the bottom porch a group of men and women sit in a row of wooden chairs. Their hands are composed in their laps and they regard the camera with level glances. No one is smiling; the occasion is the funeral of my grandmother's father; the widow sits in the center of the group, sagging a little in her heavy black dress. My grandfather, who is an outsider, a country boy in a starched collar, sits more stiffly, more grim than anyone else. His bride lifts her chin, half turns her head: she has married a boy, if you compare him with her sisters' husbands, who are heavy, neckless fellows and have stores in the parish seats. One sister is a beauty, with dark hair and slightly protruding eyes. She married a fat man. "He shot two men in Memphis on Hester's account," my grandmother said. She said nothing more — she had never been beautiful. There is a handsome brother, too; he was a wealthy man who liked to steal. He cheated my grandparents out of my grandmother's inheritance, and for that reason they left the parish altogether. Years later they heard the house had been torn down. When my grandmother looked at the picture, she would rub it with her thumb.

"There's Betty," she would say, and point to the corner of the house where a black woman with a plain dress and long apron stood on the dishevelled grass. I used to think that Betty had just wandered into the picture, had come round from the kitchen and discovered, to her surprise, that a photographer was there and the family lined up on the porch. But now I think that she had been told to stand there in the grass beneath the porch. "I loved Betty like my own sister," my grandmother cried. Once my father said that Betty had been shiftless and frightening, and my grandmother came to my mother in tears: "How can he talk that way about Betty? We loved her *so.*"

"They treated those Nigras like they were part of the family," my father used to say. He meant to say it proudly but it came out sounding uneasy — for he and his father too had chopped their own cotton once upon a time. "The Munroes treated those Nigras . . ." The Kellins, presumably, had looked across the rows and seen somebody else's blacks walking to work. My father had no time for his mother's photographs. "The Kellins were prosperous people back in Virginia," he said once, and I realized that he was quoting his father — the only time I heard him do this without derision.

The Kellins had wandered south out of the Tennessee mountains, bringing only their odd name and stories about lost plantations, and although my father never spoke well of his father, he has spent some little time tracing the family history — perhaps to justify the Kellins to the ghostly Munroes. A few years ago he told me a story about his efforts. He had been in St. Louis, and looking in the telephone directory, he found the name "G. M. Kellin." He thought about it for a while and then he dialed the number: "It was the doggonedest thing — this woman answered and I introduced myself and said I was in town and I was always interested in the family history and thought it was just possible we might be related. I tried to be discreet about it, you know, I didn't want to impose myself on these people. Well, darn it, it turned out she was a colored woman. A very highly educated respectable colored woman. Her husband worked for the government. She was very nice about it but she was embarrassed and said she didn't think we were related, her husband got his name from his grandfather who was a slave back in South Carolina. We talked for a little while. She was pretty nice about the whole thing. Sounded like a highly educated woman." He told me this story several times, and he always began by saying, "Did I tell you this doggone thing that happened in St. Louis?" Telling the story made him nervous, but he said he thought it was funny.

Fifteen

After dinner we took Leona home and then drove back down to the beach. We parked the car and took off our shoes and walked to the edge of the water; there was a moon, and the ocean was very quiet.

"I can see a ship," I said.

"They've made imitation islands out of the oil platforms," John said. "Off Santa Monica. They cover the derricks to make them look like buildings, they even put up fake palm trees. People call to ask if they can rent apartments on those islands."

"Too bad," I said. "Oh, but look at the ships."

"Those are drilling platforms," he said. In a fairy ring of moonlight at the horizon: three brilliant jewels.

"I wish I could go out there," I said, but I couldn't, and so instead I turned lunatic with wishes and ran along the beach, through the thin lappings of the water, through darkness and blinding wires of light from the highway to darkness again. That was the pier ahead, those were palm trees at my right hand — I looked through them to see the mountains, indistinct as fate. Then I turned to see John standing where I'd left him, and so I walked back to him.

"Are you living with Cabby?" I asked.

"No."

He put his arm around me and we walked to his car and we drove a little ways to his house: a cottage in the *barrio* where all the houses were small and poor and clumps of flowers stuck out of dirt packed hard and smooth as a floor.

He had four chairs in his house. I sat on one and watched him pour two glasses of brandy.

"You don't have many things," I said. "But all of them are beautiful. You live like a saint."

"I don't see any reason to have ugly things in the house. You betray yourself that way, you know. It's something I don't understand about you."

"You mean I buy cheap things," I said.

"Sometimes. You waste your time . . ."

"Maybe I don't know any better," I said. "You were always waiting for me — I thought — to *snap out of it*. To change *for the better*. I always thought, *he's imagining how we'll live on a ranch and work very hard and* — *be virtuous*. You know."

"I never said that. I wouldn't ask you to do that if you didn't want to."

"But I ought to want that! That's what I think!" I was frightened; my knees were shivering under the table.

"Are you going to stay with me?" he asked, and sighed,

and held my hands. After a while he took off my clothes and I took off his clothes. But then, touching each other, it was as if we began to speak in another language — in itself absolutely clear, without nuance or irony, but at the same time incomprehensible — like a language so strange as to be unidentifiable. And so you listen and imagine, make words from sounds, begin to translate and then let it go and at last accept that it has no meaning: a simple, formless music. Then it was quiet. I heard a mocking bird. I felt John's hot body lying next to mine, growing cool.

"What did you say?" he said.

"Oh. I said, Oh." I was looking at the floor. A column of ants had climbed into an empty brandy glass, and now they were taking the lees away, a molecule at a time.

"I'm going to buy a ranch," he said.

"How?"

"Cabby's giving me the money. I'm going in with some other people — the guy teaches at the university. I'd like you to meet them. His wife is a terrific girl. She makes candles."

"I bet she bakes her own bread."

"Don't be a bitch."

"Of course I'll like her," I said. "So I've got to say bad things about her before I meet her."

"I don't care if you don't want to bake your own bread. I don't care if you don't even want to cook. You could do what you like." He sat up, arranging the pillows behind him, his chest a pillow for me. "Wouldn't you like to try it? If you didn't like it, you wouldn't have to stay."

"Right," I said. "That doesn't make me much of a pioneer woman, does it? Like when I get bored, I just run back to the city."

"Maybe none of us'll stay. We may hate it. Fuck it. We'll sell it. Everything changes. Change with it. I'm buying the

33

ranch because I want to find out some things. I don't know what I'll do when I've learned what I want to know."

"I can't afford it," I said.

"Why don't you ask Leona for the money?"

"Ah," I said. "Why don't I ask you to let me in for free?"

"Sure," he said. "But I know you. You wouldn't like it unless it was your very own."

"Yes," I said. "You're right." I got out of bed and put on my clothes. "Would you mind taking me back now?"

Sixteen

The next afternoon it was hot. Leona had cut irises and put them in the dining room, and their heavy scent filled the house.

"I wish I'd brought something for Eddie," I said to Leona.

"He shouldn't expect it." She twisted around to look at the back of her skirt. "I'm sorry, dear, but I'm just going to wear what I've got on. I don't see any point in changing."

"What time did he say he'd call?"

"Around four."

Eddie would be over forty, probably grown bald, and he wouldn't wear a zoot suit or drive a Crosley. He would not recognize me at all, yet undoubtedly we would search each other's faces for resemblance, even lie about it, to make this reunion plausible. But as I paced from one room to another, staring at every chair and table as if *then* or *then* or *then* the sound of the doorbell would explode in my face, I began to wish that it were all over with and he were already gone again, taking the puzzle of our meeting with him. It grew clear how foolish it was to think that we would have anything in common — or only just enough to prevent us from becoming as intimate as strangers seated together on a plane. On the flight from New York I'd sat next to a businessman — he must have been about forty — who had just left the savings and loan game. He gave me his card; it revealed nothing. "I spent ten years in Cleveland," he said. "And I consider 'em all wasted time since I've been here."

"Yes," I said, "the heating bills, the schools."

"No, my wife's relatives," he said. "Never go into a family business, it never works out." Every day, a friendless, friendly commuter, he took a plane to San Francisco or San Diego or Los Angeles. He rented cars, he took his meals in the terminal buildings. Even as I was standing in Leona's dining room, he was probably somewhere in the sky above me, drinking orange juice.

I looked at the clock when it was quarter to four, and a few moments later the telephone rang. I kept pacing until Leona appeared.

She said: "He can't come. That's what he *said*. I told him, wasn't that a little bit thoughtless of him? I'm sorry, I know it isn't my business, but after all he was coming to see me as well, and I could have gone to town this afternoon instead of waiting here." She sat down with a great show of stiff joints. "Honest to goodness, I think it's plain rudeness. Don't ask me what he said right now because I'm too mad to think about it." Her head was trembling, but finally she spoke again: "He didn't explain. I asked him if he wanted to talk to you and he said he thought you'd be too busy and I said you surely were *not* too busy but he wouldn't all the same."

I didn't understand.

"I'm sure I don't either!" she cried. "I said well then what did he want to see me about."

"What?"

"Bunkum."

He had, it seemed, asked her about our grandmother's estate. He had also asked her not to mention his enquiry to me, but she thought I should know about it — she had told him so, in fact. Then she had gone on to tell him that she knew very little about that business, since "that family" was always very close-mouthed about these things, but as far as she knew, Mrs. Kellin's will had distributed everything, and "everything" was mostly furniture, among the four children . . . or so she imagined, since she had never heard another word about the will. ("And I tell you this, young lady, that as a friend I knew how your people, your father too, went on about any unfairness in money matters.")

"Finally he said it, flat out, that he thinks there was some money in *trust* for him."

"Is that possible?" It sounded crazy to me.

"It's not at all possible. These things are a matter of public record. He doesn't have to talk to anybody. He can look up the will all by himself."

"And the will's in Santa Barbara, isn't it?"

"It should be." Leona hated to talk about anybody else's money and now she was squirming with disgust.

"Do you think I should look at the will?"

She gave a little cry. "This is all bunk! He's making a fuss for nothing. Your people are the most honest people I've ever known. And I'll tell you another thing and don't you forget it, miss: this is some idea somebody else has put into his head. Some cheap lawyer sent him up here. I know what I'd say to a fellow like that!"

I thought about this for a while and then I said, "I'm sorry I didn't see him."

"It's not your fault."

"He must be crazy," I said. "There's no trust fund. There's no money."

"Well, you're like your father. You're sensible about these things."

"I am, aren't I?"

"Let's have a drink," she said, taking advantage of the crisis. This led to a lot of going back and forth and finding glasses and deciding what we'd drink and wheedling ice cubes from Mrs. Gomez, who got into the spirit of the occasion and winked and giggled and produced secret stores of macadamia nuts, cheese biscuits, and potato chips. "Pip pip," Leona said. "That sun is right in your eyes."

"Cheers. I'll move over here."

"John is a lovely boy, isn't he," she says, testing the wind.

"We've known each other a long time."

"He's very fond of *you*, I think."

"It seems that way."

"Mm." She smiles, checks a button between her breasts, irons her hem with her fingers.

"You could work out here, couldn't you?" she enquires.

"In Los Angeles."

She gives a little honk: a gasp. "Los *Angeles*." But she means to be game about it: "Where would you *live?*" as if nobody in Los Angeles *lived* anywhere, merely dwelt in their cars perhaps.

"I could get an apartment. With a pool." Why not?

She uncurls a smile, lets it snap back, to show she appreciates a joke. "That's how my boy died, you know." I know: at thirty-six? thirty-seven? he dived in, drunk possibly, cracked his skull. He had meant to marry again, have a child this time. He'd said so; he was just relaxing between marriages when he sprang from the board: getting in shape.

"I'm sorry," I say.

"Oh, everybody has them," she says. "I used to be quite a swimmer."

37

She seems to want to go to sleep; her body wilts as she drinks, her hands drowse in her lap.

"If you wanted to stay on here," she says. "I could see to it that you wouldn't lose by it. I'm sure you're making a nice salary now and you don't want to give that up, but if you wanted to rest for a while . . . oh, you know what I mean. *I don't need a nurse.* But this house is big enough for two people, we wouldn't get in each other's way. And that way you wouldn't have to pay for an apartment, you could put something aside. We might even take a little trip together. I don't know whether I'm up to it, but if I felt like it in a few months I wouldn't mind seeing Italy again. If Helen had lived — I promised her I'd take her to Italy."

"I've never been to Italy."

"It's *very* beautiful."

"Thank you," I say. "I wish I could go with you, but I have to get back to work. Why don't you go with Mrs. Galleon?"

"She fusses. She gets worse all the time. She can't go out the door without a coat and a scarf and gloves and what have you. I don't even bother to ask her to meet me for lunch anymore. 'Oh, Leona,' she says, 'I'll have to get ready. I'm afraid it's too cold. Is it windy? I won't go out in the wind.' She drives me crazy." But Leona is proud; she snaps upright, wraps her arms together. "I'll just go by myself," she says. "American Express will have to take care of me."

"That's the spirit," I say, and immediately I am ashamed, sad: speaking to her as if she were locked away in a ward. The visitors' day voice: That's the spirit! Keep smiling!

"You wouldn't lose by it," she says again. Now we're talking business. Her eyes are cool as nickels.

"But you would," I say. "I'm very expensive these days."

"What have I got to spend it on?"

38

"Who knows? I'm sure you can think of something."

She agrees with a nod. "It gets spent somehow," she says. "Never ending." She gets up — perhaps she is going to take an inventory, double check the grocery bills, sell the house. "Never ending," she says.

"Where's Eddie staying?" I ask.

"He must be gone by now": not without satisfaction.

"I'd like to see him."

She thinks the motel is called the *Mar Vista* or *Vista Del Mar* or *Vista Marina,* and as I study the Yellow Pages, she offers me her car for my troubles: "Don't smash it into a tree. Be careful going out. There are lots of streets without stop signs up here, go slowly. Some people around here drive like they own the road."

Steering the Lincoln backwards down the drive, I glance toward the house to see her worrying at the window, like a sailor's wife: will I founder, be becalmed, drown?

Seventeen

We are very much alike, I said to Eddie — alone: I had a lot to say to him before I saw him. Nothing could be misunderstood, yet; watching the street, I imagined he was sitting beside me. I'm sorry, I haven't got the hang of this. This car is like a ship, isn't it? I was nervous because the steering and the brakes worked absolutely, but he said nothing. *I'm not reckless,* I apologized. He didn't mind. *This car suits you,* I said. You looked so gallant years ago. I can't quite remember, it was the way you held your head, I think: it was something special to be young and blond. Everybody looked at you in a certain way; they couldn't keep their eyes off you. That was the reason I never thought until now that you and I were alike. I always thought: *Well, he is thinking of something else.* As I might think of a rare and beautiful bird, *it is thinking of something else.*

Yes, his silence said, yes, he understood. He was as pleased as someone in masquerade — what is the pleasure of the mask, after all, if recognition doesn't follow? It was you all the time!

The blocks of houses were going by too fast — I had so much to tell him, still, before we met:

I know what you're after. I understand, even if other people don't. I know there's nothing mean in it. You haven't come here because you're greedy. I wish you were successful. I wish there were a legacy to be taken freely — rightfully yours, and mine. Couldn't we make some use of it? It would be as if we were trusted. Blessed. It would be ours by right and by chance too. We lived too close to the rich when we were children; we saw how the source appeared as if by chance — and now we're looking for the source again. But it isn't here. Our lot is merely just, merely fair. We're rewarded for virtue, punished for sin. Let me tell you something: when I come here I'm relieved for a while. It's not what I want after all. The weight of desire falls away. Do you understand? Do you feel it too? Are you relieved that there was nothing to be gained? Let's have a drink on that and be kind to ourselves and praise each other: our foolishness has a limit and our wishes haven't killed us.

We can go back up north together. We can drink beer with our father and eat Mexican TV dinners and fight about politics and tell stories and think that we are, willy-nilly, a family of sorts. We don't have enough people to love, you and I; but there is a legacy for us, after all — those wives, husbands, mothers, fathers, uncles, aunts, brothers, sisters. I've found you, Eddie. I've found what I came for.

Joy makes ugly streets beautiful: joy finds gardens, trees laden with fruit, fresh paint. Joy believes that signs speak the truth: Welcome! Rest! Vacancy! Pool! Free Color TV! Joy delights in wishes — this might be *El Rancho*, or *Avalon* or *Shangri-La*. *Vista Del Mar*: it would, if it could, look at the sea. But it could not. Yet one was Welcome there too, and charged very little. The office was full of pictures and brochures, as if to say: you don't have to stay in these little rooms from morning to night. Sleep here, and then go away to see beautiful and amusing spectacles. The woman behind the desk wanted to know what she could do for me. I wanted to see my brother. She looked through her cards: she was happy to tell me he was staying in number fourteen. We looked out the window together. His car was there.

As I walked toward his room I wondered if he saw me: the blinds were lightly drawn on his window. Unseen, he could study me at leisure. He could decide, if he wished, not to open the door; and I thought, I don't have to knock. I can walk away now. The television set was going inside the room; he would never know if I walked away now. *You are always running away*, I told myself. There was no time to decide whether it was true or not. I lifted my hand to rap at the door and was glad it was so easy, a muscular habit, for if I had to think to raise my forearm, to curl my fingers, to draw my hand back and fling it forward, draw it back, fling it forward —

"Just a minute."

I meant to speak first, but my mouth was too dry.

"Who is it?"

"Margaret," I said.

"Who?" A tall, thin-faced man opened the door. He had thin, pale hair. He wore gold-rimmed glasses and a short-sleeved green shirt and gray trousers and he was standing there in his socks, holding a copy of *TV Guide*. Then I saw that he was Eddie, and then he looked exactly as I'd remembered, although until I saw him I hadn't realized how clearly I remembered him.

"Margaret?"

I put my arms around him and discovered that he was stiff and trembling. He hugged me too tightly, then his arms sprang away.

"I didn't want you to leave before I saw you," I said. The words sounded to me like wa-wa-wa-wa. "I wanted to see you so much."

For an instant he looked completely bewildered and helpless, and then he stepped back, not too far, but far enough to show me that I'd forced my way into the room, that it was a dim, ugly room. There was the print of his butt on the chenille bedspread. One of his shoes, its toe curling up a little, stood on the floor between us.

"Well, you didn't give me a chance to clean the place up!" he said. "You caught me by surprise!"

"I'm sorry."

He gave me a look and then straightened the bedspread, turned off the television set, and put on his shoes. His fingers worked strangely at their tasks, as if they had never done anything with pleasure. When I sat down he stood up, went into the bathroom, and closed the door. After a couple of minutes he came out again, smiling triumphantly, wearing a sports jacket and a necktie. "I'd better look my best for an occasion like this!" He had a way of pausing before certain words and pausing afterwards, as if placing them in quotation marks: "I'd better look 'my best' for an 'occasion' like this!" He grabbed my hand suddenly, almost painfully. "This calls for a 'celebration!'"

"I think so too," I said.

When we stepped outside the air was pink — that stroke of dusk peculiar to dry, hot cities, when the shadows soften and all things glow for a moment. The street lights are on; the sky has paled from blue to mauve. At this hour objects lose their solidity. On the highways pale cars smash into each other. The survivors wake in darkness, as if from a pearly dream.

"Where is your car?" he asked.

"Over there." I pointed at the Lincoln. "It's not mine. I can't drive it very well. Do you want to take yours?"

"Oh, I understand," he said. "Do you mind if I take a look at it?"

First he walked all the way around it, and then he bent to look in the windows. "A lot of people will tell you that this sort of car is a waste of dough," he said, "but I don't agree. They're superbly engineered. If I could afford it, I wouldn't have any other. If you take care of it, you won't need to trade it in for three or four years. Oh —" he winked at me "— that is, your friend the owner. Mine isn't nearly as well built as this one, but it's a very decent car for people in my income bracket. It's astonishingly reliable for a medium-price machine."

"I don't know anything about cars," I said. "I remember I thought you —"

"Well, you don't need to know anything about them," he said. "A pretty gal can always find a fellow to advise her about these things."

I made myself smile, and it was a reflection of his: pinched and deliberate, like a smile for a photographer. We walked back to his car, an ordinary blue American car. He started to get in, and then he got out again and walked around to open the door for me.

"Where are my manners?" he said. "You'll think I'm not

used to going out with hep chicks. But you know, the gals are so independent nowadays, some of them are offended if a fellow opens the door for them."

"I'm not," I said. "Thank you."

"Thank you!"

He thought we would go to my favorite night spot in Santa Barbara, and when I said I didn't have a favorite place, that I'd been away too long, he said he bet he could find something up my alley. This was still a city for the "wealthy few," he added, giving me a knowing glance, and he knew a place that was good enough to compare with anything in New York. The place was The Seven Seas: a Polynesian confection of flaming gas torches, fishnet, tapa cloth, floodlit electric waterfalls under plastic bamboo. I liked the trickery-fakery of it. "It's wonderful," I said.

"I knew you'd appreciate a sophisticated atmosphere," he said.

A waitress in a tiny sarong came to take our order; Eddie asked for an Outrigger for me, a ginger ale for himself. The waitress paddled away. He lounged very deliberately in his chair, working his fingers. "They won't let you in a joint like this without a jacket and tie," he said proudly.

"You don't want a drink?"

"No, but you mustn't feel like a loner on my account. Liquor does not agree with me. After I went on a couple of benders many years ago, I decided that it didn't have to play a part in my life. Thoughtless people sometimes urge you to take a drink, but if you're firm with them they'll generally drop the matter. Your drinking set doesn't want to waste the hard stuff, after all." He laughed a good deal at this. "In places like this of course they are disappointed if you don't have two or three stiff ones. They make an enormous profit that way. They could not afford this fancy decor if they didn't serve the booze. People like myself get the short end of the stick: we can entertain ourselves for little dough, but the surroundings are pretty humdrum."

"How's your mother?" I asked.

"She's not very strong."

"I saw our father in San Jose," I said. "He seems to be in good health."

"He has always been good at looking after himself." He stopped smiling for a moment: "How is your mother?"

"Fine."

"I liked her very much," he said. "She was a 'superior' personality. There was nothing of the condescending about her. It was relaxing to be around her."

"They may get divorced again," I said.

He turned his head a little, as if he wanted to ignore this. He began to make a soft humming noise: mmm-mmmm-mmmm.

"I hope it doesn't happen," I said. "She's scared to be left on her own."

"Here's your drink," he said. " 'Bottoms up.' "

"I have not been very close to the rest of the family," he said. "I am not sure if this is an accident or by design. It occurs to me that my personality did not fit their criteria for a jolly good fellow: in any event, it has been made clear to me over the years that my absence from 'the clan' has not particularly concerned anyone. At one time this was a source of hard feelings, but as you grow older you learn to take these things as the facts of life. Obviously you have the sort of personality 'the clan' finds congenial. It has proved to your advantage. I wish I had the knack! It is evidently natural to you!"

"I don't understand."

He began to make his humming sound: mmm-mmm-

mmm. Then: "Well, you evidently want to make me feel at my ease by pretending there is no great difference between us."

I don't know. Is there a great difference between us?

"It is certainly a characteristic of our so-called democratic society that persons of wealth take care never to acknowledge that they are set apart from the rest of us."

"Eddie," I said, "I'm not rich."

Mmmm-mmm-mmm.

"There's no money, Eddie. I live on a salary. I wish there were lots of money. I wish there were secret trust funds and things like that, but there aren't."

"It is clear to me that they have put one over on you, then, Margaret, and I'm sorry to see you haven't managed to secure your 'rights' in this matter. I wish I were in a position to give you sound advice, but as you see I have had no great success myself, hah-hah-haha! Well, you are well set up in the meantime, and for someone in your tax bracket it is probably better to let sleeping dogs lie."

"*There's no money. Nobody in our family is rich anymore.* I don't know where you got this idea, but it's wrong. I hate to see you making yourself unhappy about it. I want us to be friends."

"Let's go," he said. He pointed at the empty glasses. "Or we'll be clipped for another round."

He walked out jauntily, smiling, humming, nodding at the other customers. "I would offer to take you to dinner, Margaret, but I am down on my luck this week."

"Let's go Dutch."

"To be honest, I don't think I could even pay my fair share at a decent restaurant."

"My treat."

"No, thank you," he said, opening the car door for me.

"You will think you've been set up to treat me. I am no gourmet! I can get a sandwich and a cup of java somewhere and be perfectly satisfied wtih that."

We drove back to his motel. "There's your car," he said. "Safe and sound. Those cars are the favored targets of boosters, you know."

"It's Leona Haggenburger's car," I said. "Do you remember her?"

"I talked to her on the telephone. I guess I roused her fighting instincts. She was pretty short with me the last time we talked."

"I could go back by way of San Francisco," I said. "Maybe we could meet up there."

"Margaret, I am sorry to have to drop a hint, but you are very persistent. I don't see that we have very much in common. You mean well, but you would soon find out that I am not part of your fast set. I don't get on airplanes and fly to the east coast when I feel like it. I do not have the sort of pals who lend me expensive automobiles. As far as I can see you are innocently aware of these material differences, but I cannot take them so lightly. I have managed to support myself all these years without welfare or handouts, while the rest of the clan lived off the fat of the land. We might have been friends once, but they have seen to it that there can be little basis for a friendship now. I wish you every happiness. Clearly you deserve it. There has been no reason for you to become embittered, as I have, and the result is a very fresh and carefree quality. I'm happy for you. Somehow you have escaped the clan's puritanical influence. You at least seem to know how to make use of your lucky breaks."

"Goodbye, Eddie," I said. "Let's keep in touch."

He kissed me lightly on the cheek, and then he ran around to open the door for me. When I was in the Lincoln and pulling away from the curb he stood on the sidewalk, looking very happy and blowing kisses at me, kiss after kiss. And I blew kisses back, feeling happy for him, because I hadn't spoiled his fantasy at all. I looked in the rearview mirror to see him standing on the pavement, feet apart, hands on hips: a justified man.

When my legs began to shake I turned off at the beach and parked between cars full of lovers. I thought I was going to cry, but to my surprise there were no tears available: as if I'd cut my wrist to find that all the blood had drained away without my knowing. I'm dead, I thought. Then I drove back to Leona's house.

She came into the kitchen while I was eating the supper that Mrs. Gomez had left in the oven. At first I was alarmed: her face was pale, her features seemed to be erased, and she was peering at me with one eye screwed shut, her hands snatching at the folds of an old robe and a gown, sickly peach colored. I could see her skull through her hair. But she had only been asleep.

"I didn't hear you come in," she said. "Is everything all right? You found your supper? Haven't you had anything to eat?"

I said everything was fine.

She shuffled closer, trying to open her eyes. She said, "That's too bad." I think she was waiting for me to start crying.

"I think I'd better be going tomorrow," I said.

"That's up to you."

"I can take a plane from Los Angeles," I said.

"All right," she said sharply, and she turned around and left me.

In the middle of a dream I can't remember, I was suddenly awakened. Somebody had turned on the light in my room.

When I sat up Leona was standing in the doorway. "Don't be frightened," she said. "Somebody was trying to get into the house. I called the police."

By the time I'd found my bathrobe, the police were in the driveway and flashing red lights licked the windows; I could hear the car radios as I went downstairs. Leona was standing in the front hall, talking to two policemen; they watched me come down the stairs.

"Does she live here?" they asked.

"No," Leona said. "She does not live here."

"Did you hear anything?" they asked me.

"No," I said.

They went outside again and I followed Leona into the living room, where she sat down in a big velvet chair.

"I heard him," Leona said, very loudly, as if she were speaking to somebody else in the room. "I heard him walking along the driveway, and then I heard him doing something to the window."

"Who was it? Did you see him?"

"I'm all alone in this house," she said. "Anybody can get in. I can't defend myself." Tears sprang into her eyes.

The policemen came back after a while and told us that they hadn't found any signs of an intruder. They suggested that a dog might have made the noise.

"I didn't hear anything at all," I said, trying to drive away their suspiciousness. Policemen reek of suspicion; they kept looking around as if to say, We know something is going on. If we look hard enough we'll find you've broken the law somehow. Something is wrong, their glances say: Why did you call us?

"Well, ma'am," they said to Leona. "Are you going to be all right now?"

She wouldn't answer.

"Ma'am, as far as we can tell, there's nobody anywhere close to your house now. You just make sure your doors are locked when we leave. We'll keep checking by for the rest of the night. But it's been our experience that these guys don't try again. That's been our experience."

"Thank you," Leona said.

I went to the door with the policemen.

"How's her hearing?" one of them asked me.

"Very good. I don't know. I thought it was very good."

"But you didn't hear anything. You were asleep, you say."

"Yes," I said. "She woke me up."

When they went out I locked the door and put up the chain. I turned around. Leona was watching me from the doorway to the living room.

"Did you lock the door?" she asked.

"Yes," I said.

"I want to see that," she said. Finally I stepped away from the door, and she came over to look at the latches. "Go to bed," she said.

"It was probably a dog," I said.

"I can't be sure," she said. "I'm all alone here. I've got to be careful."

She looked at me so angrily that I could feel my head begin to tremble: I wanted to kill her.

"I thought it was your brother," she said.

"I don't think it was, Leona," I said. I started to go up the stairs very fast, and then I began to run, and finally I was in my room, pulling out drawers and wadding clothes into my suitcase. I could hear her come to the door.

"Margaret," she said. "Margaret. Please answer me. You must answer me! *Don't you be like this!*" She opened the door and came in.

"Margaret," she said. "Why didn't you answer me?"

50

"You heard a noise," I said. "And you immediately thought it was Eddie. Well, what am I doing here?"

"Don't act like a fool," she said. "I'm sorry."

"I'm sorry too," I said. I went over and put my arms around her; she smelled sour with fright. "It was just a noise," I said. "Nobody was trying to get in."

When she left I got into bed again and turned off the light; I could hear her walking from room to room, latching the windows. After a while the sky began to pale and the voices of the birds rose in the dewy darkness. Then I got up as quietly as I could and finished packing and washing, and finally I called John and said, *I have to go now.*

Eighteen

John said he would take me to Los Angeles, but he wanted to start early so that we could go on the back road through the mountains. Leona came downstairs and told Mrs. Gomez to fix breakfast for us, and afterwards she came out in her dressing gown and stood in the driveway, giving critical looks to the gray sky and the flower beds that were not yet raked. When John started the car she pounded on the door and cried, "I want you to come back soon!"

"Did you see your brother?" John asked. "What was he like?"

"Like a brother," I said. "I probably won't see him again."

"I'm sorry," John said. "Do you need a brother?"

"He doesn't need me."

"What about you?"

"Oh, John," I said. "I have everything I need."

The plum-colored Mercedes rolled through empty streets

and gray light. For a while it joined the commuters on the freeway and the tractor trailers with their lights still on, and then we turned off into the mountains, winding and climbing past orange groves. At one bend in the road we met a bobcat; he glanced at us and then ran into the brush.

"Come to the ranch," John said.

"Wouldn't that be nice. Maybe some time —"

"Why don't you say *no* for a change?"

"All right. No." Then I knew he wouldn't ask me again.

After a while we began to talk; we had said everything of importance, and we were left with gossip and dreamy silences. The car came to the top of a mountain, the sun came out, and below us lay a lake and empty pastures. We started to sing:

> *Put another nickel in,*
> *In the Nickelodeon,*
> *All I want is loving you,*
> *And music! music! music!*

We knew only one verse, but we sang it again and again, louder and louder, as the car flew down the road.

Somewhere north of Los Angeles the road curled along the side of a hill that was covered with live oak and tall yellow grass, and as I looked at the hillside I saw something black shining in the grass. The road was narrow and we were moving very slowly at that moment, and so I got a good look. There was a stream of oil running down the side of the mountain. Some place on the slope a pipeline or a pump had broken and the oil poured down through the grass in a thick, shining course toward the road, where it fell into a ditch and followed us for several hundred yards. I was so fascinated by it that I almost forgot to tell John what it was until it was too late, but he saw it too. I remember I said, "Look! It's a river of oil! I thought it was a creek but it's oil! It's so beautiful! beautiful!" The sight of the oil made me tremendously happy, and ever since that morning I've remembered it and it still makes me happy to think of that stream of oil pouring down the hillside through the dead yellow grass.

Nineteen

My grandfather left his wife's parish after his father-in-law's funeral and took his wife and four little children to another part of Louisiana. He bought a farm, and for years they lived on the food they raised themselves and the scanty profits of their cotton and hogs. My grandfather was happy, I think, because he was a curious man, and he'd try feeding his hogs peanuts one year and cottonseed the next; he'd take off with his shotgun to explore the countryside, and he invited strangers to the house for homemade beer. But his children hated the farm, and from this I guess that their mother hated it too. Every summer until my father was ten or so my grandmother would take the children back to her home town and lead them through the respectable parlors of her mother's house.

As a consequence the children left home as soon as they could. The girls got married and the boys took up trades that would bring secure income. Then two years after Robert, who was the youngest, lied about his age and joined the army, someone discovered oil on the farm. The Sewannee-Beaulieu Corporation leased the land; the cotton and peanuts and popcorn and my grandmother's flower beds disappeared under gouts of oil; and that year my grandfather moved them all to Santa Barbara. One of the oil company men had told him that Santa Barbara was a swell little town. When I was little I used to sneak into my grandmother's desk to look for pictures, and I saw the buff-colored envelopes with an orange sun printed in the corner and the big black letters: SEWANNEE-BEAULIEU. Once my mother tapped the desk and said, "Almost a million dollars went through that desk!" but I already knew the money was gone. The envelopes were empty and they had old stamps on them. My father says that every year he still gets a check for ten dollars or so from the company; the old wells pump just about enough oil to run one used car, he says. He laughs.

Once I drove across the country and saw, in western Kansas, oil pumps working on the plains. They look like big iron grasshoppers with their heads bobbing up and down. I liked to watch them, and I didn't mind that they were in the fields because I knew that someday the well would dry up and all the oil would be gone and the weather would rust away the iron. Meanwhile they were something alive and purposeful in the empty plain.

Twenty

Last week I read Leona's letter again about the oil in Santa Barbara, and I wondered what it looked like — would it float up to the beach in one huge mass and cover the sand, or would little slicks drift in, a few at a time? A magazine had pictures of it, and I cut one out. It shows a man standing in the water and holding up a dying bird. You can't tell its species. It had seen a fish glinting through a wave, I suppose, but when it dived to seize it, oil flowed over the surface of the water and clung to its feathers, and it couldn't fly away. The oil companies have promised to rescue as many of these birds as they can.

Part Two

A Lot of Cowboys
and Other Stories

A Lot of Cowboys

When it began to snow all the cowboys came into town and rented motel rooms with free TV. One of the cowboys said his favorite program was "Bonanza." "It's pretty authentic."

"Aw, shit, what do you know about authentic?"

"Well, I know. I'm a cowboy, ain't I?"

"Well, so am I, and I think 'Bonanza' is a bunch of bull-pucky. Now if you want authentic stuff you ought to watch 'Gunsmoke.'"

"Well, you old cuss, I will show you what's authentic." So the cowboy hit the other cowboy with his fist.

"No fighting in here, so you cut that out," said the motel manager.

"You're right," the cowboys said. They got some ice and some White Horse and some Coca-Cola. The motel manager said to his wife, "By God, you can't tell them dumb cow-hands nothing. They mix good scotch with Coca-Cola."

"I knew I never wanted to marry a cowboy," his wife said. "I knew *all* about them. They weren't the fellows for me." She was keeping her eye on a young couple who weren't married; the girl seemed to have made a wedding ring out of a gold cellophane strip from a cigarette package. Looked mean; good thing the poor fellow hadn't married her yet. That night in the bar the motel manager's wife told him he shouldn't marry her.

"Huh?" he inquired.

A number of cowboys went to see the Ford dealer. He turned on the lights in his office and brought out two fifths of bourbon. The cars stood around the showroom like cows around a campfire, reflecting little gleams from the office and little gleams from the street. You could almost hear them sighing.

"Goddamn, that Maverick is a pretty little car," a cowboy said.

"Yeah, yeah," another cowboy said. "But I tell you, I got my eye on a pickup so pretty you'd like to cry. Dark-green gold-flecked. Air conditioning. And I'd hang toolboxes on the side. And maybe —"

He had their attention.

"— and maybe I do and maybe I don't know a Mexican fellow who wants to make me hand-tooled leather seat covers."

"Aaaaoooooow-*ha*. WooooooooowwEEEEE."

Also little tsk-tsk-tsk noises. Head shakes. Lip bites. Breaths indrawn.

"Pwuh," said the Ford dealer. He was a classicist. He couldn't stand to think of a hand-tooled Mexican leather seat cover. Of course he was a town fellow.

"When I was in the Army," one of the cowboys said illustratively, "I got me a tailor over in Munich, and I went in and I said — well, I drew him what I wanted, and he made me a suit, *bitte schön!* Mama, oh that were a suit! It had six slantpockets in the jacket. Course, uh, course, I don't wear it too often, you understand."

Oh, yes, they understood!

There were those cowboys laughing like they were fit to be tied.

An old woman living above the Western Auto store stuck her head out the window and listened to the cowboys come and go. The snow was falling slowly, and down the street Stan Melchek was sitting in his car waiting for a speeder. A pair of lights appeared in the distance but it was a big tractor-trailer rig, after all, pulling slowly through town, and its tail-lights went past the All Nite Truck Café, and the old woman pulled her head back inside and closed the window.

One cowboy lay on one twin bed and another cowboy lay on the other. One cowboy said, "I like Tammy Wynette. I sure get a kick out of her. My favorite record is 'Stand By Your Man.' My little sister sings it just like her. You close your eyes and you don't know it ain't Tammy Wynette singing. She wants me to get a guitar and learn to play and accompany her."

"I wrote a song once," the other cowboy said. "I showed it to this fellow works in Denver, and he said maybe I could publish it and maybe I couldn't."

"Oh, there's money there," the first cowboy said.

"Oh, you better believe it."

"What's on now?"

" 'Hawaii Five-O.' "

"Shee-it."

"Well?"

"We sure as hell ain't going to no drive-in tonight."

We had all these cowboys in town because of the snow, and they were mostly drinking whiskey and watching television and talking about cars. It was Saturday night, but you sure couldn't tell it from any other night because of the snow. The Basque Hall advertised a dance, but the group they were going to have didn't have chains or something and anyway called from Salt Lake and said nothing doing, so there wasn't even a dance. Some of the older fellows went to the motel bar and danced, but it was mostly Guy Lombardo, which the bartender's wife favored. Maud, the motel manager's wife, had different ideas; she sat down next to a cowboy she knew and said, "We need to light a fire under some of these old cayuses. Play some of the music the kids like."

"I don't like it," the cowboy said.

"Well, hell, no, *you* don't like it, an old fart like you. Hell, you can't dance that way with one foot in the grave."

"Now, cut it out."

"I'll wash out my mouth, Carl."

"I don't like to hear you talk like that, Maud." His eyes filled with tears. "Honest to Christ, Maud, you was the most beautiful girl I ever saw. You wore your hair the sweetest little way with two little curls in front of your ears, and you wore a green silk dress. You were the sweetest little thing."

"Now, don't start crying here."

"Well, God help me, I can't help it."

"You'll just make me cry too." She had handkerchiefs for both of them. She got another round of drinks. That mean little thing with the cellophane wedding ring was looking, and Maud bet *she'd* never known a real man like Carl. These cowboys were always getting drunk and bawling, and it made her bawl too, to tell the truth.

So, you see, everybody was either in a motel room or in the motel bar, and it was snowing pretty heavily, and then George Byron Cutler drove into town. He was something of a celebrity because his picture was up in post offices, and he was known as G. Byron Cutler and Byron George Cutler and G. B. Cutler, to give only a few of his aliases. He was wanted mostly for mail fraud, but he had also held up a post office and was armed, and considered himself dangerous. He usually wore khaki shirts and trousers, but he wore good boots.

Most criminals have a peculiarity like that. Anyhow, George Byron Cutler went to the motel and asked for a room, and then stuck his head in the bar and yelled, "Where's the action?"

"Well, now, I thought you was bringing it," somebody yelled back.

"Well, I was, but she didn't have a friend."

"Well, bring her in."

It kind of fell flat. He winked at Maud.

"Is my old man at the desk?" she yelled.

"Yeah, your old man is at the desk," said a voice behind George Byron Cutler. And so Cutler went on to his room, and about an hour later two sheriff's men came by and said they were looking for him.

"Christ almighty! I got to tell Maud," her husband said. "Don't you do nothing 'til I tell Maud. She won't forgive me if we got a bandido in the motel and she's not here."

"You done us a favor," the sheriff's men said, agreeable. They accepted a Coke apiece. They left snow on the Astroturf. "That's Astroturf," Maud's husband said.

"God almighty," the sheriff's men said.

So Maud's husband went in to get Maud, and she said real loud, "You mean we got a criminal in this here motel? Oh, I don't know why this hasn't happened before. We are the only motel for fifty miles. The only motel you'd stop at, that's to say. Of course there's always Mrs. Oldon's place. You boys don't stop there, you hear?" A lot of coarse laughter greeted this remark, because the cowboys knew that Mrs. Oldon had a prostitute come through in the summer. Every summer she had a different prostitute, and these girls were known as Winnemucca Discards. It was a common joke that only sheepherders went to Mrs. Oldon. "I am feeling like a sheepherder tonight," a cowboy would say, and the reply to that was, "I'd get a sheep instead."

"What sort of a criminal is this fellow?" Maud asked.

"He's a mail fraud," her husband said.

"Sounds like a pansy to me," a cowboy said.

"I want to see the police capture him anyways," Maud said. She rose to her feet, showing a lot of bosom to the assembled, and led the way to the motel lobby, and all the cowboys and even the mean girl with the cellophane wedding ring and her "husband" followed. The sheriff's men were feeling the Astroturf.

"Snowing like all hell," one of the sheriff's men said.

"Is this fellow dangerous?" Maud said.

"Well he is armed and considered dangerous," one of the patrolmen said.

"He's in 211," her husband said.

"Then everybody can see," Maud said. They all looked outside and saw the two layers of rooms, and 211 was pretty well located, being close to the big light and close to the middle of the balcony. The sheriff's men told everybody their names and shook some hands and then went out while everybody watched from the lobby. They went up to 211, and you could see them knock at the door. They didn't even have their guns out.

"He can't be very dangerous if they don't even take out their guns," Maud said.

"It's a Supreme Court rule now," somebody said.

"I don't know how they catch anybody."

Then there was an awful sound like a board breaking and nobody knew what it was at first and then one of the sheriff's men started yelling and all the cowboys and everybody else started yelling, "He's been shot! Jesus Christ, he shot him! Oh, get out of the way." The other sheriff's man started running, and then 211 opened the door and George Byron Cutler stood there with a gun in his hand.

He was shouting something but nobody heard it. Finally a cowboy lying on the Astroturf slid open the double glass door and yelled back, "What did you say?"

"I said I just want to get out of here," yelled George Byron Cutler. "I have killed a man, and I have nothing to lose now."

"Did you hear what he said?" Maud asked somebody. "I would never have featured it."

"Where is that other sheriff's man? Did he shoot him too?"

It turned out the other sheriff's man was back in his car calling for help. And all the cowboys in the motel rooms were calling to find out what was going wrong. Maud got on the switchboard and told everybody, "Don't peek out. God almighty, don't peek out. Just keep your door locked and lie low. He has a gun, and he has killed a police officer."

George Byron Cutler walked toward the lobby with his gun shaking. All the cowboys and women were on top of each other on the floor or crawling away, and a lot of people were crying. Maud said to the switchboard, "Dear Lord, he is coming in here. I got to hang up now. Do not come here. You cannot help us."

Then George Byron Cutler tried to open the lobby door, but it was cold and stuck. He began making faces and pounding at it. "Wait wait wait wait." A cowboy got up real slow and opened the door for him.

"Just stay as you are," Cutler said to everybody. "Give me your money."

"I'll give it to you," Maud said. "But I haven't got much cash."

He thought a long time. Then he told everybody to throw down their credit cards. He took the whole pile of credit cards and put them in his shirt and said, "This will take some time to work out, boys."

Later Maud said she'd thought at first he was scared but he surely showed he was a cool customer.

Then he went out again and they heard a car start and make lots of noise and roar away, and then they heard some more shots, and finally somebody went out and found the cowboys from the Ford dealer's place all standing around the street where George Byron Cutler was lying dead, shot by Stan Melchek.

"I thought at first he was a speeder, but when I stopped him he fired his gun at me."

"I guess you didn't tell him his rights," one of the cowboys said.

"Oh, shut your mouth," another cowboy said. "This fellow has been killed."

Nobody could sleep after that. Maud opened the coffee shop and heated up some bear claws. She sat down with Carl and a couple of the younger fellows.

"Stan Melchek is a cowboy," she said. "He is a cowboy by nature. Those fellows shoot first and ask questions later. That's the code of the West. These big-city criminals don't realize they're out in the Wild West. Out on the frontier here."

"They don't realize," Carl said.

In a very sad voice Maud said, "Well, I guess he learned."

"You don't fool around with a cowboy. You don't fool around in this country," Carl said.

"The cowboy is a vanishing race," one of the cowboys said.

"But he's not finished yet," Maud said.

"Not by a long shot," said one of the cowboys.

Twice Plighted, Once Removed

Dr. Kovotny said, "All you need is practice," so I put up a sign: "I'll Listen." At ten o'clock the buzzer rings; I go into the hall to see who the cage is bringing up. It's Dr. Kovotny. "This won't cost you anything," he says, putting a limp hand into my welcoming one. "Where can we talk?"

He runs through his troubles; not unlike mine — I wonder if he's borrowing some of mine. Then he runs through his patients' troubles. But I haven't had much practice yet, I'm already tired of listening. "Tell me your troubles!" I cry.

"I have an illusion," he says, inaccurately. "It's lovely. When I lie in the bathtub I imagine the water is filling the whole room, covering the fixtures. Shuts out the noise. My patients pound on the door. Come in, I say. We can't, they say. We can't swim. Then I say, That's too bad! I alone am happy."

"Very hard on your patients," I say, full of self-pity.

"*Tant pis,*" he says. "Nice place. You could fix it up more. How much do you pay for a place like this? Eighty? No? Rents are going up all the time. Listen, if I made two thousand more this year every *penny* would go back to the government? You ought to know that kind of thing." He has run through my package of potato chips, and now he has the door of the refrigerator open. "Don't you keep any *snacks* around? What's this — yogurt? That's all nut stuff."

"You're supposed to be taking care of me!"

"Okay, okay, talk to me office hours. You got any bread for this?"

"I'm supposed to be practicing listening right now," I say firmly. "I might get another client."

"You can't listen to two people at once? Where's a knife?" I'd never noticed before that his pants cuffs ride a little high on his ankles. He has thin ankles. Maybe he has small feet, but they're hidden in enormous brogans. When he turns around he's licking deviled ham off the corners of his mouth. "My wife is a terrifically sexy broad," he says. "She's all woman. You get what I mean? Not like these kids. Going around in tight sweaters, showing off their boobs. They haven't got any boobs. I don't want my kids to grow up seeing that kind of thing."

"Please go home, Dr. Kovotny," I say.

"Whatever you say. Baby."

Then I went to another analyst, but he wouldn't believe me about Dr. Kovotny. He said it was my fantasy, and he asked me to repeat the story several times. "Look in the phone book! Call him up!" I said. The other analyst came in one day and said he'd talked to Dr. Kovotny and looked at me very severely.

"*I'm* not a liar," I said, and I wrote him his last check.

"Why is it so important to you to make me believe you're honest," he said.

Oh, well.

I was born to tell somebody else everything. My mouth is a loudspeaker: continuous live coverage of birth, pain, joy, hate, sex, greed, envy, gratitude, bewilderment . . . My parents fled to their automobile. My brothers and sisters refused to read books so that they would not have to understand me. At my first confession I acted like it was first communion and I pounded into the booth overflowing with sins, misdemeanors, tricky questions. The priest wouldn't look at me. "I forgot about my parents," I whined when he tried to buy me off with a negligible penance. He forgave me; in his person God told me to Shut Up. Then I started telling everything to God. I said, "You've got to listen. That's what You're there for. Let me tell You about my plan for turning salt water to fresh water." God tried to tiptoe away. I pursued Him with candles. I'd go by the church in the evening and surprise Him.

"I know You're in there. I want to tell You how I felt when I hit this boy in the seat behind me."

Finally God just went away. I'd say, "Let me tell You how I'm feeling tonight," but when I listened, all I could hear were the molecules banging together, like one of those beaded curtains after somebody's passed through.

At a certain age I began to have boyfriends. "Now tell me about *you*," they'd begin, unwisely. After a few boyfriends the same old story grew stale. I varied it; I began *in medias res;* I lied. Finally I could not bring myself to tell it again, and that boyfriend beat me up. "Talk to me," he said. "You never talk to me." So I told the same old story again, weeping with boredom. "You should see a psychiatrist," he said as he scrubbed at my tears. What a good idea it was. Thereafter I talked to psychiatrists and went to bed with fellows smart enough not to ask me any questions. "Will I change if I tell you all this?" I asked the psychiatrists. They were, to say the least, noncommittal.

Dr. Kovotny was not the first to tell me I should listen. "To whom?" I said, that first time. I went out in the street and started to listen, but nobody was saying much. Mostly they said, "Hi! How are you! Good to see ya! Look out there! How much is this? Do you deliver? Do you carry the *Nation*? I haven't been doing much lately, just goofing off. Haven't seen much of the old gang. Keep in touch." Why should they want to keep in touch, I wondered.

After Dr. Kovotny and the guy who thought I was a liar, I tried to listen to the Great Americans. I snooped in Emerson's diary to see what he had to say.

"The towns through which I pass between Philadelphia and New York make no distinct impression," he said.

Thoreau said, "Winter has come unnoticed by me, I have been so busy writing."

Henry James wrote a letter and asked, "Is the egg crop failing?"

"I haven't been doing much lately, Henry," Emerson probably said. "But keep in touch."

My own life has grown more and more uneventful. Things happen, but it's like yarn: you knit and then unravel and when you start to knit again the wool is kinked, it bends itself into the same old stitches. So I've become shameless about borrowing other peoples' lives: "Tell me what you're doing!"

They think I'm listening.

What I'm actually doing is collecting things to tell. Ida's miscarriage is scrubbed clean of names and passed on to Sally. Sally's dandruff treatment is passed on to Lily. Lily in her turn supplies a fight in the upstairs apartment and a phone call from her mother-in-law. No disservice is done. On the contrary, I am practiced at telling everything, and when I retail the story of Rose's adultery, I have added small details, turns of phrase, nuances of emotion that were knocked off in the story's troubled passage through reality.

To Rose, her last rendezvous with Tommy was dreary and anti-climactic. They got in his car. They drove to the Arboretum. He said he was worried about the children. She was at a loss for words. He drove her back. She and Bill went to the Wigwam that night.

I am the one, not Rose, who remembers that she wore a pink straw bucket hat with anemones on it — a hat she didn't like, but she was thinking of throwing it away when Tommy called. And I remember that Tommy puts his handkerchief over the phone when he calls her and tries to sound like a salesman in case Bill answers. "Good afternoon, is this the Bonner house!" he says loudly at the beginning of each adulterous conversation. Rose gets him off the line quickly; her sister is in the John Birch Society and says all the phones in the country are tapped. And I remember that Tommy takes her to the Arboretum because he doesn't like nature, and he can't imagine anybody else — except Negroes, whom he believes to have a kind of natural affinity with nature — will ever go to look at a tree. (In fact, he has said that Negroes don't go to look at trees either. He believes they have secret ways of hunting small game and harvesting wild plants in city parks: he admires their self-reliance. I can't imagine where he got this — it must be something he remembers from a book he read when he was a child in Minnesota.) And I remember that Tommy worries about the children because he is afraid of his children, and with good reason: they are two tall boys in the armed services who would "take him to the cleaners" if they heard he was playing around. And I remember that when he drove Rose home he went right up into the driveway to "put Bill off the scent" and Bill saw him and for the first time in two years became mildly suspicious of Tommy's intentions. At the Wigwam that night Bill pressed Rose against his bosom and said he knew for a fact that Tom Ohm likes a good time, and Rose was thrilled.

Ah, Rose, forgive me.

In the days when God was listening, I used to say, "Say only the word, and my soul shall be healed." Now who's to say it? but I believe it — one true word, one good spiel: the carnival barker does almost as much, why can't I? Rose, let me try again:

You sat in a frayed canvas chair on the lawn behind my house. You wore white imitation leather sandals, pale nylons and a lemon yellow linen dress with three white buttons at its throat. You also wore your wedding ring, your engagement ring, and a platinum ladies' watch your older boy, George, had brought you from Germany. Your no-color-straw-color hair stood straight up from your scalp, pulled up, teased and lacquered by somebody's determined comb. Your lips were only flecked with color: you bite your lips when you aren't speaking. You were trying to make a funny story out of your guilty conscience.

"Let me have another drink," you said twice. "It gets funnier."

You had always meant to be decent to your husband. I have seen you looking over his shirts from the laundry and you stopped cooking lamb and then "fried foods" because he said they didn't agree with him. But maybe you wanted a reward for decency. You said once:

"We were strict with the boys, but I think they'll thank us for it later."

Why should they? They grew up to be bullies, gossiping about other peoples' weaknesses at the table, interfering in arguments between you and Bill. I was in the car with you one day when the older boy came over and leaned on the window and said, "Mom, don't let him do that to you."

"Do what?" I said.

He gave me an angry look, he didn't have to say it: none of my beeswax.

They sent you enormous gilt-framed photographs of themselves in uniform. You wanted a cuckoo clock.

I was not astonished when you told me you had gone to bed with Tom Ohm. He is a nice-looking man, not better looking than Bill, but different. Anybody who ever looked at you, after all, said: Guilty. With that look. Some of the pleasure was having something to confess, at last, after the years of unconfessable sins: letting Bill bore everybody with his lectures on the ill-effects of "fried foods," idly encouraging the boys' vanity and their malicious gossip. Watching television instead of reading books. You name it: your face has lines on either side of your nose that say No, no.

But your eyes are hyacinth blue and shiny like tiny, tiny lakes: no dead women have eyes like that. You said you were worried about Bill, his dad had died when he was fifty, but we know that you will die someday too, whether you are decent or not.

Don't you want to protest?

Rose, you are a nihilist at heart. When you want to talk about something of value, you talk about your mother's silver service; but you keep it locked in a safe deposit box.

"Of course they'll blow up the banks one of these days," you said. Nobody listens to you, so it doesn't matter what you say.

What is there of value in your own keeping? Everywhere you listened and looked they said *love*. Keep it, give it. Love is a treasure. You know better: you do the shopping, after all. You found no real worth in it. Soon I expect you will join a church. You like your drinks, but you would exchange them for any real coin.

"Let me have a cigarette," you said. "Let me tell you about the Arboretum."

I listened as closely as I could. Now who will listen to me?

This afternoon a letter arrived from San Diego. Lily is out there. Her husband works all day. Her infant is inarticulate. The neighbors have one story which they pass around and around: a teen-age boy robbed the corner grocery store and got away with two hundred and seventy-four dollars. He has not been captured. To me Lily writes, "Keep in touch."

Evenings Down Under

A middle-aged fellow who looked like he knew what he was talking about came on television in the afternoon to speak to us. "Many of you have asked — how long do we have to put up with these conditions? You want an answer. You are no longer satisfied with the usual answers. You want to know what is being done." That was all he said that afternoon, but it made sense to me.

I said to my wife, "Yes, that's what I want to know."

She replied, "Yes, I have the same question."

It was a great relief to have heard that fellow speak as he did. For the first time in a long while I felt like my old self, and I undertook several tasks that I had been postponing. My wife does not say much on these occasions, but she has a way of letting you know how she feels. Time passed more quickly than usual. Some of our friends dropped by.

"Did you hear that fellow on television?" Leland asked.

"It was a relief to hear some sense spoken," Marietta said.

"I would give a dollar to hear more of the same," said the older Mr. Stanley.

"Plain talk's the answer," Mrs. Stanley said.

"Not just talk," my wife said.

"That goes without saying," Leland put in.

It is hard to believe that things can get much worse. I have heard some say that it was worse in the old days, but I am no judge of that, and I do not think you can altogether trust to memory in these matters. What I know is that everybody I know has been affected by the present situation. Some of course do not discuss their troubles, but they have troubles just the same. It is clear from the faces of strangers that there is no general sense of well-being in the air these days. My wife complains that there is rudeness wherever she goes, and although I do not encourage her complaints — for it seems to me they only aggravate her distress — I could match them with stories of my own. We are no worse off than anybody else of our acquaintance, but nowadays this is no reason to congratulate ourselves.

After supper I told my wife I thought that fellow might be on television again and I wouldn't mind hearing some more of what he had to say.

"I feel the same way," she said.

"You're not the only one, I'm willing to wager," I told her.

When she turned on the television set there was the usual stuff to be seen — that's why I don't watch television very often, to be honest.

"No wonder," I said to my wife, and I pointed at the screen.

"I don't wonder at all," she said. It was plain she didn't like what she saw. I hoped that fellow would come on again soon, if he was coming at all, because I was in no mood to watch the usual stuff. We did not have to wait a long time, I'm happy to say. The usual program was interrupted, and that fellow appeared on the screen.

"Since I last spoke to you I have received many telegrams and telephone calls," he said. "I wish it were in my power to answer every message personally, but this is not in my power, and so let me say only that each telegram and telephone call has been received. But I want to say that even if I had received no response to my first remarks, I would still be speaking to you again tonight.

"You are tired of asking questions. Asking questions is your right, let there be no misunderstanding about that. But now you are demanding another right: to have your questions answered.

"You understand the present situation as well as I do. It is not a matter of understanding the present situation. Anyone can see that conditions are bad. Anyone can see that things are getting worse. Anyone can see that something needs to be done. It is no use pretending otherwise, particularly at this late date."

That was all he said that night. It gave us something to think about. I said to my wife that a little sense was better than a lot of nonsense. She said she looked forward to this fellow's next speech.

My neighbors agreed with me.

"He knows what he's talking about," said the older Mr. Stanley.

That afternoon everybody waited for the fellow to speak again. We were not disappointed. He looked the same as he looked the night before, wore the same suit, sat in the same

76

position with his hands folded in front of him and resting on a table or desk. He looked straight into the camera. I don't believe he was reading what he said; his eyes looked right into my eyes and he seemed to be saying just what he had on his mind, not what he thought would make a good speech.

"There are no easy answers," he said, right off. "There is no cure-all. Things are being done. Things have been done. But there are no easy solutions.

"Of course there are always short-term solutions. Many problems could be solved immediately if we contented ourselves with short-term solutions. Many problems could be solved immediately if we chose the easy way out. But we want long-range solutions to long-range problems. We do not want to put off until tomorrow what we should deal with today. It is no good taking care of the present and letting the future take care of itself."

Afterwards my wife said that she didn't think she understood what he said. She asked me if I understood what he said.

I replied, "He is dealing with very complicated matters. It is no use trying to simplify these things."

"Yes," my wife said, "you're right."

"We can only wait and listen," I said.

"I guess so."

Although I did not say as much to her, I was disappointed by his last speech when I thought it over. It is too much to hope that problems can be solved overnight. An easy explanation is as bad as no explanation at all. He said we understood the situation as well as he did; if that was so, I should have known that he would not try to insult our intelligence by offering a simple analysis of complex events.

"There has been too much oversimplification," I said to my wife. "We now have to face facts."

Some of our friends admitted they had lost confidence in that fellow. I was sorry to hear it. They got no satisfaction from admitting it.

"I would give a lot to feel otherwise," Leland said.

"I imagine you would," I said.

"I am not saying I have confidence in anybody else. If I had confidence in anybody at all, it would be that man. You can be sure of it. It isn't easy to give up. He is right when he says there are no easy solutions."

"I wish I could persuade you otherwise," I said to him.

"So do I," said Leland. "I have time to spare these days."

"I know what you mean," said Mrs. Stanley.

"It's not at all what I expected," said Marietta. "I remember, when I knew I had passed on, the first thing I said was, 'Well, this isn't what I expected.' I remember I laughed at the time, I was that surprised, you know. I expected it to be old-fashioned, you know. Fires and things. But now it's so unfriendly and odd, you don't know what to expect. I would have done differently if I'd known."

"Well what do you expect?" said Mrs. Stanley.

"What indeed," said Marietta. "He gives us something to talk about." It was hard to know just where she stood on the matter.

The man on television said: "There are those who claim the people have a right to know. But I want to say that I believe they have other rights as well. People have the right to know, but they also have the responsibility. There are more impor. rights than the so-called right to know. That is not the right that is being violated nowadays. People have the right to know *something*. They have the right to know that something is being done. That is more important than the right to know. They have the right to know how long they will have to wait until something is done. That is more important than the right to know. I know you would rather know that I am doing something than know what I am doing."

When he was finished I went into the kitchen. My wife was poking in the drain with a straightened out coathanger. I said to her, "I wish you had heard that fellow just now."

"I'm sorry I missed it," she said.

"It doesn't matter," I said. "What matters is that he said it. To be honest with you, I don't understand everything that he says. But I don't have to understand everything he says to know that he knows what he's talking about. There aren't any easy answers. It is no use expecting them. But sometimes it is good to hear it said plainly."

"I wish I had heard him just the same," she said. "It is better than nothing."

"I'll let you know when he's on again," I told her.

Leland and Mrs. Stanley came to the house after supper and proposed a game of cards. I found a pack with fifty cards in the sideboard; Leland said fifty cards would do if we couldn't find a full pack. "It is better than nothing," Leland said.

"I thought Hell would be like this," Mrs. Stanley said, while she was waiting for her cards.

"You were right," my wife said.

"So I was," said Mrs. Stanley.

The Mother of Good Fortune

When I was six years old my mother left my father, and she took me to another city to live on expectations. She had been a handsome and quick-witted girl, the secret darling of her family, but they also had lived on expectations — that they would inherit money from a rich uncle or a brother's ranch, or have a clever son — and so when my mother was married twice and twice disappointed, she left her husband to go someplace where once again she could wait for her fortune. But to wait, and to receive nothing, had become a habit of life for her, and even though she could not say this to herself, she believed that she had received unhappiness for her share; her life had failed, she had lost her chances, and she did not believe she could make it good by her own will. She did not even have a son, someone in whom she could place her hopes as her mother had; only a daughter, who was moody and talkative, already damaged by the broken marriage.

It was a prosperous year when she left my father, and with a little money and some lies she managed to buy a house. She had not wanted to do this; she had wanted to do as her sisters had suggested: put me in a boarding school and find an apartment and a job for herself. But the school proved to be an unlucky choice, for I was mistreated there. I was too stupid and frightened to complain, but during Christmas vacation my mother happened to ask me if I was anxious to get back to school, and I said no, that the women there teased me and humiliated me and told me that my mother didn't want me. My mother was humiliated by this, then, as well. She did not send me back to school, and within two months she found a house and a public school where I could go in the daytime.

The house she bought was really too large for her means. When she had spent what money she could, she found she had nothing left to make a proper lawn or buy enough furniture or a refrigerator. In the neighborhood of the house the young husbands, who had been in the army, took great pride in their gardens, bought secondhand cars for themselves and their wives, wrote letters to the city government demanding pavements and sewer systems, and devoted all their attention to their homes and their children. I could share this household affection; I was included in all vague, enthusiastic invitations to the children at large to share a picnic or a marshmallow roast, and now and then my mother and I found ourselves in the back of a crowded station wagon headed for some park or unfenced countryside. My mother looked in the newspapers for public outings: picnics for families from Iowa or Ohio, Baptist or Catholic socials, civic excursions. She took me to these and made friends for the afternoon, for she was still clever and handsome, and her failure made her ready to agree to any opinion or praise anything another person took pride in — but afterward she would mock the people we had met.

I became unhappy whenever I measured the difference between our house and the houses of my friends; and even though these children came to visit all day, I was afraid and ashamed that they would notice that the furniture was secondhand. We did not have a car to take the other children on picnics or trips to museums (but my mother would take me and one or two others by bus), and after school I made the long walk with her to the market and then walked back empty-handed because she would not allow me to carry groceries. I suspected that my friends came to the house because my mother was less strict than their own mothers, and I became very animated and pushy so that they would come for my sake alone; but reflected in my mother's open gaiety, I saw myself changeable and awkward. The only excursion I enjoyed wholeheartedly was going to the movies; the only theater close enough to walk to was a drive-in, but they kept some benches in the front for people without cars, and on warm nights we sat together in a darkness that smelled of dry earth and looked up at the enormous screen with its enormous voices.

When I was ashamed or unhappy, my mother felt it like a splinter under her nail — the shame especially, since she had fought against her shame of herself for so long. She gave me whatever I knew how to ask for: a paper-doll book, a plastic toy, praise; but I did not know many things to ask for, and at times I stared at her with a look of dumb greed, which frightened her because she recognized a greediness like her own for something we could not name. These moments passed and returned and passed again, and meanwhile night after night we sat across from each other at the supper table, talking in a lively, courteous way like two strangers who have struck up an acquaintance on a bus. I liked this companionable relation best; of all things in our lives, it alone gave me a sense of being a solid, separate person. For a time I convinced myself that she was not my real mother but a woman who worked with a group of kidnappers, and hoping to find some clue to this conspiracy, I continually asked her to tell me stories about her life and her family. She liked to tell these stories. She did not even mind telling them again and again. Sometimes she sang me to sleep, but I was afraid of the song she liked best, and the words gave me a stifled feeling:

> *There's a long long trail awinding*
> *Into the land of my dreams*
> *Where the nightingale is singing*
> *And the bright moon beams.*

I always believed that the song was about her brother who had been in the war.

My mother looked for work, and although she had gone to college and had been trained to do several things — had in fact worked before marrying the second time — she now had no confidence in herself and avoided jobs suited to her experience. She made excuses for herself: that she did not have a car, that these jobs were scarce and demanding and badly paid in this city, and that they would leave her too little time to take care of the house and me. Instead she sought whatever appealed to her at the moment: temporary jobs or work that seemed to associate her with "interesting people." She told lies to get these jobs, lies far too complicated even for her to remember. She would work for a few weeks at a time and then tell another lie that would allow her to leave; increasingly she urged herself that we needed little more than the money her husband sent for my support. She had not asked for alimony. Out of pride she insisted that we were really well off, that we had easy expectations of my father, and that he was in fact generous if he was tricked into being so. Money would come as certainly as a ripe apple from its branch. Sometimes I used all this against her and wrote to my father, asking him to take me away.

My mother had wealthy friends who spent the winter in a hotel in the city: Agnes and Harry Fay. She had known them since childhood. They had been poor when they married, had worked hard and bought land. After the war the land became very valuable and their business prospered. They had a beautiful daughter, Betty, who had just finished high school, and they had lots of friends who had become rich as they had in the same boom times; every few weeks they would call my mother to ask her to dinner or to a party, and they would find men to go with her. She became attached to a man who could not marry her, but despite this, and despite the fact that I made fun of the man (I called him "the pumpkinhead" because he had red hair), she was happy in her own way for a while and believed that at least the expectation of some little change had been fulfilled; but then the man left the city, and just as she was reconciling herself to this, a Diesel truck ran over Harry Fay and killed him.

At once my mother was eager to help, and she threw herself into the macabre excitement of her friend's troubles. The beautiful daughter was turning crazy and abusive — they must conspire to stop this. Old friends were trying to buy the business and the land at a loss to the widow — she must encourage Agnes to take over the business alone and make a go of it. Her friend was foolish with grief and terror — she must be made to see the good that surely lay ahead. All the force of will that she could not use for herself, all the force that would taint the purity of her own expectations, she could find on her friend's behalf. Many mornings, even school mornings, my mother carefully dressed herself and me. She put on her best suit; and instead of the blue jeans I wore to school, I wore my best plaid skirt, a freshly ironed blouse, and my Easter coat. Agnes Fay gave us money for a taxi, and we would ride to the hotel where she had stayed on after the funeral, the taxi driver outwitting the hesitant and shabby secondhand cars that belonged to the neighbors and people like the neighbors on their way to work.

The hotel was old and grand — not in any absolute sense, but in relation to the city, which was new and gaudy — just on the point of decline, like a coin tossed in the air, pausing, about to descend. That year a larger, more modern, and more ostentatious hotel had been built on the other side of the downtown area; but all the money in town was new money, and those who had just had time to settle into the old hotel were waiting for a while, testing their fortune, and enjoying the chance to mock the newest money that went straight to the newest hotel.

In the morning, men in carefully cut ranchers' suits and hand-stitched boots would go down to the coffee shop, then buy the papers and sit in the lobby, where large and mis-shapen leather chairs were placed shoulder to shoulder around the imitation Spanish pillars. The bellboys and clerks here still made as much in tips as those in the new hotel, but here they had to know the names of the men who tipped them, and there was a ritual of good fellowship, compounded of gifts of whiskey and financial advice from the guests and the appearance of ingenuity from the employees: "I know as where I can get that little thing for you, Mister Bolam," a bellboy would say. "No need of you goin' around there. I was just on my way out to get this fellow in 218 a bottle of aspi-rin. No, don't give me any money. I always have to carry money. I'll trust you, Mr. Bolam. Isn't everybody I'd say that to. Just you wait a minute." And the bellboy would return with a watchband or undershirts or a bookie's receipt or the telephone number of a clean girl.

When my mother entered the lobby with me, she straight-ened and drew in a little breath of relief, as if she were stepping off a train into a town where everybody knew her name. Years before, between her marriages, she had insisted that her beaux meet her in the lobbies of expensive hotels; she would arrive early and finish combing her hair and settling her collar in the rest rooms of such hotels, where there was always a colored woman in uniform and gold mirrors, and then she would go out and sit on some wine-colored chair, smoking and secretly studying women's dresses and the faces of the men. Now, here, she was known as Mrs. Fay's friend, Mrs. Windus, and when she crossed the lobby she smiled at faces she recognized, acknowledged the stetsons touched for her, and led me past them with fussy motions of her hands. I was always excited by this progress, and it was not until we were inside the elevator and my mother was chatting with the elevator man that I realized that I dreaded these visits.

As we turned along the corridor, the image of Agnes Fay's daughter, Betty, came into my head: a fiercely pretty brown face and shoulders drawn up and a hard, drawling voice, "Didn't your mama ever tell you you weren't supposed to mess with other people's things? Get out of there!" I had opened a closet where there were party gowns and a fur coat and jersey dresses embroidered with pearls, and I had been pulling them out, wrapping their skirts around me, when I was caught. After that I brought crayons with me and used the hotel stationery to draw pictures of princesses, but this was dangerous too, since once when Agnes Fay showed Betty a drawing of mine, Betty made a face and said, "Swell. Listen, I could draw too when I was her age. I won a *prize* at Immaculate Heart, if you remember." My mother told me that Betty was unhappy and confused, but this only made me hate her the more.

In fact, the excuses my mother made for Betty Fay were rare and simple compared with the excuses she made for my presence. She did not let me go to school, since she would not be at home when I returned (and she knew that I was bored in my classes); and she refused to hire baby-sitters — she said that she could not trust them, that they might frighten or neglect me, and she was proud of her singularity in this attitude. But once in the hotel suite, once faced with her friend's easy welcome, she was obliged to apologize for my coming, and for a few minutes she would admonish me to be good, not to roughhouse or get into things, not to interrupt or disturb so much as a pile of magazines. Some of these warnings were impossibly strict, and others were unnecessary and curiously unreal, as if she were not talking to me (I was usually quiet and careful around adults and avoided their conversation) but to some violent and noisy little boy. If a third person were present she might even speak of "the children," a habit she had fallen into when speaking to strangers; but this falsity tormented me into speaking: "*What* children? *I'm* the only children!" "Teasing, teasing," my mother would say, and catch hold of me affectionately, a thing she never did when we were alone.

One morning when we arrived, Agnes Fay was sitting on the bed, where she sat usually, although there were chairs and even a sofa in the room. I found some stationery and started drawing princesses; my mother sat on a footstool beside the bed. At once they began to talk about the untrustworthiness of Mrs. Fay's accountant, and my mother brightened in the fullness of her malicious distrust — made jokes, told anecdotes, quoted magazine articles more or less to the point, casting all this at her friend's complacent and unlettered suspicion.

"I'm just a farmer's daughter," Mrs. Fay would say, "but I know a crook when I smell one."

"There was an article, I forget where —"

"I don't need to read any articles to know that fellow's a crook. I knew it the first time he came in looking for Harry, wanting to get an advance on his salary because of family trouble. Family trouble and a new car. Everybody's got family trouble. I told Harry. But Harry had a soft spot, you know."

"Harry never never let anybody down, Agnes. Never in his life."

"I know that — who'd know better than me?" Mrs. Fay began to cry. She took my mother's hand. "Not like these sons of bitches, they're always looking for a little easy money, they couldn't do what they're doing if Harry were here. It's the rottenness in people where they treat a widow and her child like that. Honest to God, I wish Harry'd taken me with him. If I didn't have Betty — there's another thing to break my heart."

"Agnes, don't you talk like that — now don't you ever let me hear you talking like that. You're smarter than ten of these dumb old *men,* these dumb horse's, well-you-know, put together, and you're going to show them. Harry wouldn't want to see you crying like this."

"Oh, the good God knows he wouldn't! But I've got to cry it out!"

"That's right, you just cry now, nobody's here but us. But I don't want them to see you crying."

"They'll never see me crying. Believe you me, they'll never see me with a tear in my eye. I'll be the cold little widow woman. I wouldn't give them the satisfaction."

The tears dried, Agnes released my mother's hand. They called down for coffee, and while they drank it, Agnes had my mother read letters from the lawyers. My mother read and commented, but it was Mrs. Fay who closed her eyes and figured in her head what mortgage payments would fall due in the next month and how much interest the bank would charge on a short-term loan.

It was, then, a morning like other mornings in the hotel — except that Betty was not there, and her absence, instead of leaving me at peace, made me more apprehensive: she could arrive at any moment, and then I would have no place to go; I would have to accept what she said about me. I drew two princesses — my mother and me. I didn't like them. I drew more. With each new sheet of paper I said: This will be the best; but I wasn't satisfied and kept drawing, and my nose ached with excitement.

At noon my mother told me to wash my face and hands and come to have my hair brushed; as a treat from Mrs. Fay, we were all to eat downstairs. When she was finished with me I sat on the edge of a chair and watched the women arrange themselves. Mrs. Fay decided all at once to change her suit, and my mother hung up the discarded garment, found a missing shoe, and buttoned the back of Mrs. Fay's blouse; then she started to adjust her own blouse, but Mrs. Fay let out a little sob. "Let's get out of here," Mrs. Fay said. "If I don't start down now, I do not think I'll make it. I don't care about eating these days, I'd just as well send for a sandwich."

"I've just got to tuck in my blouse," my mother said.

"Never mind. Nobody's going to look at us anyway. Hell, I wouldn't dress up for those sons of bitches down there."

"You're right, Agnes," my mother said, but she was close to tears of disappointment: it was one thing, she thought, to be careless of expensive clothes, another thing if the clothes were old.

"That old suit," Mrs. Fay said. "You should buy yourself a new one; make Arnold send you money for it. I'm fat, but you'd look real pretty if you'd take some time for yourself."

"It is an old suit, I don't know why I wear it," my mother said in a strained voice. "Come over here, come here, let me fix your hair," she said to me.

"You fixed it!"

"Let it go," Mrs. Fay said. "She looks fine."

"She can't keep it in place. I won't let her go downstairs with her hair in a mess. I won't disgrace you, Agnes. She's a good little thing, but these children, they won't stay still." She snatched at the brush and at me and began to brush my hair with short, painful strokes. I felt her anger and disappointment in her hands, and I began to whine.

"I'm going ahead," Mrs. Fay said.

"We're ready right this minute!" my mother sang out, and pushing me ahead of her, she followed Mrs. Fay and meanwhile furtively adjusted her jacket. In front of the elevator I looked at my mother and said, "You're crying."

"I'm not crying, honey. I have something in my eye. See. Right here." She whispered and bent close to me, pushing at her eyelid with her finger to demonstrate the nonexistent mote. "You be good now. Don't upset Agnes."

"I don't want to eat lunch," I said.

"Well you just sit and pretend like you do. I don't want to eat lunch either."

In the elevator she said fiercely, "They'll write this hotel up for a magazine someday," and Agnes Fay, hearing the tone and not the words, frowned. "I just said this hotel will be famous someday. What a historic old place it is."

"They'll all be going over to the Skyhouse one of these days," Mrs. Fay said, and then to the elevator man: "You too, Joe."

"I'm too old for it, Miz Fay."

"Harry always said you were our best friend in this hotel,

Joe," Mrs. Fay said, and with wet eyes she led us off at the mezzanine.

On that floor there was a private club: a small dining room, a bar, and a third room where there were slot machines and poker tables. My mother liked to eat there with her friend, for entrance implied that one knew the people who ran the city. Here my mother walked more self-consciously, and when she spoke, it was in an artificial voice. Here she believed she was ashamed of nothing and that she recovered for a while the attentiveness and pride she had felt before she was married; but that attentiveness and pride, like this, had always sprung from shame and a fierce desire to surprise them all, her parents and their neighbors, with her luck that would be better than theirs or her brothers'. I saw stiffness and anger, too, in my mother's look.

"Do you want a drink?" Mrs. Fay asked.

"I guess I'll have something. One drink at lunchtime and I get tight as a tick, but let's say this is a celebration."

"I thought old Joe was going to bawl when I told him what Harry said," Mrs. Fay said with satisfaction.

"They all loved him, Agnes."

"I'm going to have a Jack Daniels and water."

"I think I'll try a daiquiri."

"Mixed drinks are too strong for me."

"You know what Harry told me, Agnes, once. He said never drink mixed drinks. Plain old whiskey and water, that's the stuff. You'll never have any trouble with plain liquor."

"Then why are you ordering that thing?"

"Oh. I didn't think I liked the taste of whiskey. But you're right."

"For God's sakes, have what you want."

"I won't change it now."

"We haven't ordered yet."

"Oh, we haven't have we! I was so carried away, I didn't notice."

I saw my mother's expression: as if she were lost but still trying to keep the other's spirits up; and I wished I had brought a comic book so that I would not have to listen — but it was likely that she would have taken it away from me, telling me just to sit and listen, listen in this sense meaning not to understand or to speak, but to seem to pay attention. Now, instead, I looked at the drawing on the front of the menu. It showed a Spanish garden at night, where a moon was rising and the silhouettes of dancers appeared in open doorways. I imagined myself there, a cowgirl, the owner of the hacienda, inviting people to a ball and appearing in their midst in a cowgirl outfit of silver cloth (shining like the plated cream pitcher on the table), with white boots and a white hat.

My mother was not hungry, but she moved her food around on her plate, lifting a forkful to her mouth when the widow looked at her. She knew that the widow would tease her for not eating, and she knew also that her thinness was something Agnes envied, even when she said, "You're just skin and bones." Agnes, however, took up the subject of her own daughter: how difficult she was, what the doctors said, what the nuns could do; and my mother kept quoting magazine articles and praising the daughter's beauty, but rather sadly, as if it were something already lost. She could not have enough of her friend's misfortunes, and without knowing it she was impatient for something worse to happen. She said to herself that she was being realistic, and that Agnes did not realize how seriously disturbed Betty was; my mother could expect nothing else, to be truthful, of this shiftless and fortunate family that had promised nothing from the beginning. My mother tore out and saved the pages on art from

Life magazine, could play *Traümerei* and a half-dozen pieces in major keys on the piano, and had taught me to obey several commands in French: *Politesse est une fleur,* she used to whisper. Agnes understood money and collected Royal Doulton figures and used the wrong verb forms. Despite the crooked accountant, Agnes did not know how lucky she was to have good, loyal lawyers. This talk of business reminded my mother of the days when she left her first husband, before she had taken a job: imagining herself a career woman, something that frightened and excited her at the same time. She would fail at that, at this. It was as if she were posturing in a room where the floor was falling. She fell silent.

Agnes Fay said to me, "You're a good little thing, minding your mother. I remember when Betty was just your age — she behaved so well. Do you want to get up?"

"She can sit here till we finish our coffee," my mother said.

"She doesn't have to sit here. Honey, let me give you something." Mrs. Fay opened her handbag, spilled Kleenex on her lap, and took out a leather purse. "Hold out your hands, honey."

I held out my hands, and Agnes Fay spilled a bunch of silver dollars into my hands. They were heavy and cold, like water from a rock.

"You can play the slot machines with these."

"Agnes, she can't do that."

"She can win me some money. Stop fussing, Connie, you're just like an old hen."

"I'll go with her."

"You sit right here." Mrs. Fay spoke to the headwaiter, and the headwaiter spoke to a man in a gray suit, and it was arranged.

I knew I was going to win. Slowly, holding the dollars

against my stomach, I climbed out of my chair and made my way through the dining room, knowing that everyone was watching me.

In the next room where the slot machines sat on a shelf around the wall, I was alone. On the floor was a dark-blue carpet with silver stars woven into the fabric, and there were two eight-sided tables covered in blue felt, surrounded by heavy chairs. The loudspeakers in two corners broadcast piano music: "Some Enchanted Evening," and then "A Slow Boat to China" (I knew the words to both songs), and the air had the electric smell of air conditioning.

By climbing onto a chair I was the right height to operate the machines. I spread the dollars on the shelf next to a machine, put one in the slot, and pulled the handle with both hands, remembering what Agnes Fay had said once about slot machines: pull slowly, count to two, and let it go. The numbers spun and clicked into place one by one. There was a *chink* of money falling, but it was inside the machine, and I lost the dollar.

When I lost a second dollar I considered going to another machine. There were six dollars left. I put the next one in the slot very carefully and then pulled the handle down fast, letting it go immediately; it flung back noisily, rattling the coins inside. The numbers were wrong. The dollar was lost. I started to pick up the remaining dollars, when from behind me Agnes Fay said, "No, you've got it warmed up, don't leave it."

I said, "Go away, go away, *please!*" because I knew I must win, and anything could be bad luck. I pushed another dollar quickly into the slot, then paused before drawing down the handle, conscious now that I was being watched. I lost the dollar.

"Here," my mother said, "you let Agnes play, honey. Agnes, go on. She's had her fun with it."

"Let her finish."

I leaned close to the machine (its hen breast, its comic eyes), whispering to it, "Come on. Nice machine. Come on, comeoncomeoncomeon," rubbed a dollar between my hands and put it in the slot; then I pulled the handle. A bell. A bell. A bell. The money inside seethed, and there was a click. Then there was a rushing sound, and silver poured out of the mouth of the machine, so quickly that I stopped breathing, and only after that did I begin to catch at the falling coins.

"Looky here, she got herself a jackpot!" the widow said.

"Look, I won!" I held out the coins in my skirt. I was a fairy-tale child with a skirt full of silver. My mother was smiling and looking around the room.

"Thank *you*, honey," Agnes Fay said. She picked up the dollars, putting them in her purse, but she left two in the skirt for me. "Come on," she said to my mother, "we'll go out and spend these."

"From our lucky little girl," my mother said.

"Remember that," Agnes said. "You're lucky. You're always going to be lucky. Your mother was lucky when we were girls."

"I won that prize when the Golden Rule had that contest, didn't I?" my mother said. "Come to think of it. Do you remember that?"

"Aren't I lucky?" I said to my mother.

"You've always been lucky," my mother said. "Ever since you were born."

Meter, Measure or *Catalogue Raisonné*

I Self-Portrait with Bay, 1909. Water colour and oil. The National Gallery.
Leaves? Body of water? Scent? Misspelled potentate? He is now 137 years old, or 85; it doesn't matter. Decades fall like collapsing wooden chairs before his inattention. His hair is countable: a couple of hundred strands, more or less. Babies and old men don't bother to look like human beings: their faces have other needy purposes. Once he was plume-y and had a lovely profile, a favorite of snapshooting women friends; no shoulders to speak of but "nice" hands. When he painted this self portrait he sat askance a wardrobe mirror, wearing a dressing gown. She (unknown) liked him without his clothes. "It doesn't look like you! It doesn't look human!" she said. And now that her prophecy's answered, nobody can remember what the last word means.
— Does it refer to that blue bit lower right, sir?
— I don't know.

II Woman of Bayonne, 1919. Oil. Collection of Doctor and Mrs. Smith.
A joke.* The subject is a smoked ham. Or "her ham" as a

---

* I am a comedian, not a humourist, he said. Colin Parts has, however, found this remark in the letters of Nathan West, an American writer.

contemporary letter attests. Her leg. Mrs. Douglas Wynham-Davies has said that he proposed a "Jack the Ripper" triptych, wishing, in her words, to get at the "bone beneath the skin." "I wasn't slim," said Mrs. Wynham-Davies. The inset photograph was taken in 1922 — the face obviously the one that haunts works II, III and VIII.

III   Landscape, 1922. Water colour and oil. Private collection.
Mrs. Wynham-Davies' face is the "cloud" in the upper middle of the painting. The small figure, lower middle, a nude male, caused a sensation in the 1929 Gimpel Fils exhibition. The detail was subsequently covered with an almost perfect circle of crimson madder tempera — an example of the pervading humor of the artist. In 1943 the crimson madder was removed, with an unforeseen decline of popularity for the painting ensuing. Asked if he plans to restore the tempera addition, he has replied:
— What tempera addition?
— The circle.
— No.

IV   My Dog Byron, 1930. Oil. Collection of the artist.
Perhaps the most controversial piece in the exhibition, Number Four seems at first look a coldly naturalistic portrait of a supine Belgian griffon, its legs raised haphazardly, against a strident green field. Further study shows, however, that the dog's "fur" has been created by countless delicate glazings. One opinion, widely accepted, is that the painting was done over a period of a dozen years — a fact that would account for the extraordinary crispness, the pointillist resonance of otherwise subdued tints. Sir Kenneth Clark has called it a "brush-wiper," and in 1950, when the artist said this paint-

ing was his favorite, critics suspected another joke,* but the nature of the joke remains unresolved.

V   Landscape, 1935. Oil. The Tate Gallery.
A tree. Its trunk fills the canvas. One presumes that the dash of green upper right represents a leaf. The bark texture, on the other hand, seems deliberately transparent. Other landscapes, now lost, are suggested by faint shadows deep beneath the glaze.

VI   Landscape, 1937. Oil. The National Gallery.
A leaf. The green permeates the canvas except for its submission, momentarily, to a strip of red: the vein.
— What sort of leaf is it? a student asked.
— It doesn't look like a leaf to me. (From transcript of symposium arranged by Colin Parts, 1958.)

VII   Landscape Number 4, 1938. Oil. Private collection. The number "four" rendered in silver foil on a field of oil rinses. This work was a *cause célèbre* when American customs officials called it a tradesman's sign and threatened to charge duty. Not long afterwards, American reporters asked why it had been given its title.
— I did not wish to paint number three,† he replied.

VIII   Woman / Pear, 1941. Oil. The Tate Gallery.
The most famous portrait of Mrs. Wynham-Davies. Welles Roentgen has written in his book of memoirs, *Without Doors,* that he raised the issue of Ingres's *Odalisque* with the artist when Number Eight was first shown:

* See II, above.
† Now the title of Helene Wendler Mahler's biography (Macmillan, 1964).

"Can't you see?" he exclaimed. "It's nothing like!" My question — which upon recollection seems not so innocent as I persuaded myself it was — had thrown him into a towering rage. He withdrew the painting from the show and brought it back a week later: the modelling on the inner thigh had unquestionably been altered (though some have called me a liar for saying so) and the whole expression of the eyes reworked.

IX   Freighter, 1942. Oil. Collection of Welles Roentgen. Obviously a joke — or at least an irony. Impasto in scarlet, middle right, has begun to crack.

X   Bottle, 1947. Oil. Collection of Lord Pell.
— In what sense is this a bottle, sir?
— I no longer know.
— Is it a metaphysical bottle?
— I don't think so.
— A material bottle then?
— Is it a bottle? Why do you say that? Why do you call it that?
— I believe it is your title, sir.
— I doubt it.

XI   Self-Portrait with Self-Portrait, 1969. Oil. The Tate Gallery.
When he asked to see the exhibition, the gallery was closed for the afternoon so that he could see it alone and untroubled by crowds. His secretary, Bob Root, whose name habitually escapes him, carried the catalogue and read aloud from it. The artist smoked a pack of unfiltered cigarettes and dropped the cigarette ends on the floor. At several points he complained of poverty and harassment by government agencies. Asked by the gallery director what his preferences were,

he said he preferred his latest work. "An artist is lucky. He gets better as he gets older. I am just beginning to paint."

Taking Chances

They said, Terrible! how could he! Then they said, We were always surprised you two lasted as long as you did. He's immature. Louis is basically an immature person. Otherwise how could he have gotten mixed up with her? What he sees in her is a mystery.

And I just said, Well . . . well . . .

It was the day I got back from Vancouver. Louis was eager to see me at the airport, and at home he rushed into the kitchen to make the drinks; but when we sat down with the drinks he began to drop long silences into the conversation, and finally I tripped over one and said, "Something's wrong."

"Maybe there is," he said pleasantly. When Louis became an adult he had noticed that he was "boyish" and so he cultivated this quality. He let his hair flop over his eye. He ducked his head when he spoke.

"Tell me," I said.

"There's somebody else," I said.

"Sort of."

"Oh, Louis! How could you!"

"You were gone all that time," he said, the stout-hearted boy. I stared at him, trying to decide if I were dealing with a felony or a misdemeanor. He kept squirming and gobbling his drink. I insisted. He squirmed. At last he confessed, with some excitement, that he had taken up with a girl in his philosophy course, that she trusted him, that she thought we were separated, that she was very "innocent."

"Did you tell her I was coming back?"

"I wanted to talk to you first," he said.

"I wrote to you! I telephoned you! What do you want me to do? Do you want me to talk to her? Is that what you want? What are you going to tell her?"

"I wanted your advice first," he said. "You're older than she is. You're more experienced."

I thought about that for a while and decided that he was letting me go — or willing to let me go, the same thing in Louis' eyes.

"I'm going to change my shirt," he said. I followed him into the bedroom. A large porcelain horse was prancing on the dresser.

"Where did that come from?"

"She gave it to me," he said.

He opened a drawer, and then he tried to close it quickly. I pushed him away, and looking into the drawer I saw a diaphragm in a fresh blue box. I grabbed it.

"What's this? What do you call this?"

"You shouldn't snoop in my drawer."

"For Christ's sake," I said. "You're giving me a guided tour." Then I ran into the bathroom, wanting to tear the diaphragm to pieces, and that's what I did, using Louis' nail scissors. He danced about outside the bathroom door saying that the diaphragm wasn't my property. "Sure it is!" I said. "You're my property too."

And then I hit him an unheralded full arm blow to the side of his head. It was a way of saying goodbye, I suppose. I knew his first wife used to hit him and that he was afraid of it, for the blows had been followed by more lethal attacks:

kitchen knives, bookends, car doors aimed at his fingers. She had even ripped up all his clothing, once, and had thrown it into the shower. When I hit him all his boyishness disappeared: he was an angry man, his face turned to ice.

"God damn you. That's it. I'm going," he said.

"Two-time loser," I said.

I began to cry, and we had a reconciliation of sorts, but we soon learned that it was all over. Louis sent me to Idaho, and while the divorce was going through I wrote the second chapter of a book on Bizet.

After the divorce I often saw Louis at parties, accompanied by the lady of the porcelain horse, who was small and brutally inexperienced. She glanced at other people through brilliant blue contact lenses with no curiosity whatsoever. She brought her sisters — one older, one younger — to parties, as if to eliminate the need to talk to strangers. Her father manufactured china, I was told, and she was very anxious to get married, although Louis proved elusive in this matter and disappeared into Quebec for weeks at a time.

My friends — and they had been Louis' friends as well — tried to find me somebody else. Charley and Betsy called me to come to dinner. Betsy served roast beef and Charley served his old school friends, most of whom were a good deal like Charley. They were all slight of build, even-tempered and scared of women, and most of them scientists of one sort or another. Charley began playing basketball and found a bunch of new friends on the basketball court, and when he brought them home to meet me I was very touched because I imagined Charley's gamely running up and down the basketball court, straining his heart to get a goal and a fellow for me. Nothing came of these dinners, and out of desperation Charley started bringing home friends quite unlike himself: there was a Welshman who turned out to be an alcoholic. There was a middle-aged fairy in the Middle Eastern studies department who talked compulsively about his mother (and who afterwards always cut me dead when he saw me on the street). Finally there was a priest, named Father Grave, who was flirtatious throughout dinner and then unobtrusively managed to let Charley drive me home alone. When Charley dropped me at my door he said, "That Grave's a pretty lively fellow."

"Charley! He's a priest!"

"Well, a lot of them are leaving the church these days."

The next time Charley and Betsy invited me to dinner I was the only guest, and injudiciously I got a little drunk and made a remark about Father Grave as the bottom of the barrel.

"For heaven's sake," Betsy said. "We've introduced you to any number of people. I don't think you want to get interested in anybody."

"I miss Louis," I said. "I guess that's it."

"We don't see much of Louis any more," Betsy said. "I got so I couldn't stand him. It took me a while to realize it, but he was always immature." What a liar: she and Louis were thick as thieves, but that week she was quarreling with him.

Spencer and Natalie invited me to dinner several times. Actually it was Spencer who invited me. "Come and take pot luck," he'd say, and then he'd call Natalie. When we arrived Natalie would be upset — always to Spencer's astonishment — and the symptoms turned up in the food. Scorched chickens, hard rice and watery gelatin came to my plate, eloquently miming Natalie's annoyance. "How's about a little nip after dinner now?" Spencer would ask. "Or anybody to play Diplomacy?"

"You two play. I've got a headache." Then Natalie dashed upstairs to her daughter, an angel in ringlets whom she seemed to be trying to keep from my sight. Natalie's voice carried down the stairrunner: "If you go out on that landing I'll smack your bottom."

Very soon I learned to bring someone with me. In retaliation Natalie arranged large dinner parties, putting me at Spencer's end of the table and my friend at her end. Small revenges on my name drifted to my ear. "Sharon's so absentminded," Natalie said once, "that she couldn't even remember your name when I asked who was coming with her."

After dinner, as we drove home, my supposed friends exclaimed over Natalie's housekeeping: hot hors d'oeuvres, immaculate sheepskin rugs for the guests to "rough it" on the living room floor, *coq au vin* and wine bought through a club, and zinc tubs full of wildly flowering plants. She showed them a paradise of housewifery, and when I offered to make coffee they noticed *The New York Times* lying on top of my dishrack and the dead cactus in the window.

A couple of weeks ago I saw Spencer in Brooklyn, and he confided — it was over, he said, long over — that he had been having an affair with his law partner's secretary all during the time I'd known him and Natalie.

"Natalie thought I was the one!" I said. "What a shit you are."

"Oh, no, oh, no. Why would I bring you home then?"

"To show — you know."

"I'd never do that," Spencer said with a big sincere stare.

"Natalie hated me."

"Aw no." And then a little later he conceded, however, that I'd sure "thrown her off the scent."

When Dan and I met we liked each other at once. A woman named Bertha Parker gave a big Christmas party and invited me and Dan and almost a hundred other people who worked, didn't work, played, sang, taught, doped, organized, joined, schemed, climbed or had breakdowns. I think that in fact if Bertha Parker had had the chance she would have tried to prevent our meeting; she didn't like either me or Dan very well and it was probably irritating to her, if she thought about it at all, that we had a good time anyway. It had been a lonesome winter for us both, and so we got married quickly and had our first baby while we were still saying, "This doesn't have to last." We'd both been married before, and by accident we'd arrived simultaneously at the point where you look ahead and see marriage after marriage stretching ahead — an expensive hobby and a lifetime of amateur theatricals.

The first time I left Dan was just before the baby was born: I went off to Idaho after I said, "I was happy there!" and prudently took the manuscript of my book on Bizet (I was on the last chapter by that time). It was frozen January, I couldn't afford a rented car, and I walked around Ketchum, Idaho, in a thrift shop fur coat and boots that were never perfectly warm. The skiing people thought I was a crazed local woman. I went to real estate salesladies and said my husband had been killed in Vietnam and that I wanted a quiet place to raise the baby; then I came close to believing this myself — I'd killed Dan with my own little psyche. He called me. I called him. We called each other and could not think what to say, then fights would start over the silences when one of us would say, "Well . . . this is costing you money."

One night I called Louis.

"Sharon?" Louis said. "Where the hell are you? It's wonderful to hear from you."

"I missed you," I said.

"I missed you. Where are you?"

"Too far away," I said: I'd realized I didn't want him to know that I was in Idaho again. For one thing, he'd paid for better accommodations when he sent me there for our divorce.

"I wasn't fair to you, Louis," I said.

"Oh, honey, yes you were. You were always fair. I've changed since then. I really hope I have."

"I was scared to call you," I said. "When I picked up the phone I thought I couldn't do it."

"I know," he said. "There were so many things we never said to each other."

"Oh, Louis, I know it."

"I love you, Sharon. I'll always love you."

"I love you too," I said, and cried big cheap tears that were as tasty as cotton candy. "Goodbye, Louis."

"Not goodbye," he said. "Not so long this time."

"Soon," I said.

I cried for a happy hour over Louis and even had room service send up a bottle of scotch. I wanted gin but gin was supposed to be bad for the baby. Scotch wasn't good for me, however. By early morning I felt sick and frightened and I called Dan, and when he answered I could hardly speak for real sadness, that was as mean as a spider in my hair.

"Dan," I said. "I feel rotten and I'm so scared."

"You're not in labor, are you?"

When I said no there was a pinging telephone silence and then he said, "Listen right now I don't care what the fuck you do but I want you to take care of the baby so come back here."

"But they may not let me on the plane!"

"Listen, kid, you got out there ten days ago. You can get back."

"I'm scared."

"You should be."

"Oh, Dan," I couldn't say I loved him; it was as if I'd had one check and I'd written it to Louis for a joke, knowing it wouldn't be cashed, and now I didn't have another. I said, "I need you awful badly."

"I guess you do," he said. And when I got off the plane in my ratty fur coat and wet boots he said, "You must be good, now. I need you too."

About six months ago, just after Patrick's second birthday, I left Dan again. It wasn't so serious this time, although Dan and I did our best to make it seem that way — his father had died, leaving him a few thousand dollars of insurance money, and Dan wanted to invest this and savings and loans in a cooperative apartment in the city, while I wanted to get a house in the Berkshires where we could have — I claimed — two pianos! two studios! Over a couple of weeks the quarrel came to include every aspect of our life: Patrick's future schools, my interest (or lack of it) in cooking, how dependent we were on our friends, the "subconscious gratification" (Dan's phrase) we got or did not get from being up-to-date on musical gossip. I can make an anthology of fighting words:

"If you're so goddamned pessimistic about the city, what have you got to live for anyway? Why have children if you think everything's so goddamn terrible!"

"I don't want Patrick to grow up to be the kind of stinking awful creeping slimy city schmuck you want to be, in your heart of hearts you want to be. Just because you grew up in Fuckoff, Kansas."

"It's my money, you're goddamned right it's *my money*. And you can spend *your* money *any* way you please."

"Fantasies! You've got fantasies about what a big shot investor you are but Dan we would be living on welfare if it weren't for your accountant! For Christ's sake he's your accountant and he's telling you you're a schmuck and now you want to 'show him up.'"

"Fantasies! You're the one who has this *fantasy* about being the lady of the manor and living out in the country and you can't be bothered to water a plant. Listen, lady, you better find some other sucker to pick up the tab for that kind of stuff. Cause this one can't swing it."

"You've got the soul of a dentist!"

"Grow up."

I took Patrick and went off to Lake Placid, and halfway there I took a good look at Patrick's face, wizened with nervousness, and wanted to throw myself off a trestle.

"What's wrong?" I said.

He would not look at the train or out the window: instead he slumped in the corner of the seat with his hands holding on to his crotch.

"Where Daddy?" he said, at last.

"He's coming."

"Daddy!"

Then he closed himself like a pill bug, knees up, head down, and began to toot: "Daddy! Daddy! Daddy!" I put my arms around him but he shrieked with anger and kicked me in the breast, and then I cried too, too loudly and with genuine pain and he was stricken with silence, as if I'd stabbed him with a penknife. The heads of the other passengers appeared strung along the aisle like yellowed paper lanterns, but what they said was indistinguishable from what the train said: a chant of rebuke.

When we got to the resort I called Dan.

"I've done a bad thing," I said. "I frightened Patrick."

"What?"

"He pulled a fit on the train, I mean a tantrum and hurt me and then I scared him because I yelled. D'you see?"

Dan breathed heavily for a while.

"We'll come back tomorrow. Is that okay?"

"I'm sorry," Dan said.

"*You're* sorry. Oh, honey . . ."

"Now consider," he said. "If you can get Patrick calmed down, why don't you stay up there a week? Maybe we can forget about the apartment for a week and I can do some work and you can *look* at farmhouses and I'll come up Thursday and we'll have a real family vacation."

"If I can calm Patrick down."

"Sure," Dan said. "That's the sine qua non."

"Daddy," Patrick said to Dan on the phone. Then I could hear Dan's voice, so curiously shrunken by the telephone, telling Patrick that he was coming up in a few days and would bring him a surprise. The notion of surprises was beyond Patrick's intellectual powers, I suspected, but his face softened a little.

It was a week of neither here nor there, a week with apprehension — as if the week had bad breath. Until Dan appeared, in the flesh, the quarrel wasn't ended once and for all, and Patrick alternated the perfect happiness of a boy with a sandpail and moods of fretfulness and contrariness. I had the manuscript of the book on Bizet to revise, but my motive for taking it along had been such a bad one (on the train I had imagined conversations with an eighteen-year-old Patrick. "Luckily, Patrick, I had my academic credential — the Bizet book. I don't know how we would have managed otherwise; your father's bankruptcy made the issue of your support an academic one as far as he was concerned"), and Patrick was so demanding of my attention, that I just thumbed magazines and went to sleep at night with the free television whining softly, all stations off the air.

About the fourth night I was there Louis called. I wasn't surprised: he called every six weeks or so and seemed fascinated by Dan. I couldn't tell whether this was incipient friendship or unpleasant curiosity. "Hello," he said. "Dan told me you were there."

"Did you talk to him tonight? Is he all right? I was going to call him later. Did he give you a message?"

"I don't know, I don't know," Louis said impatiently. "I'll be up there tomorrow."

"Oh, Louis, how silly! I'll be back in a week. But then what makes me think you're coming to see me?"

"I am coming to see you."

"Oh, Louis." I hoped he was going to pledge eternal love again — and I needed eternal love from somebody: Dan wouldn't be arriving for three more days. "Tomorrow, then," I said, plucking the conversation in the bud. "I must go now," I said.

I went to the hotel's hairdressing lady, a soft-bosomed ex-WAC who was in business on the mezzanine with two basins, two driers, a budgie and a philodendron. She pulled my hair and rolled it, baked it, sprayed it and back-combed it into a bell shape, lacquered to a chiming hardness — just right for Louis, I said to myself, and anyway Dan would prefer it to look more natural, as it might after three days' wear. Up in our room, later, I hammered at it for a while with a brush and then "tried on" a pansy purple wrap-around and then did my nails and then ordered a bottle of brandy. From time to time I looked up from the late show to admire myself in the mirror.

"Oh, Louis," I said to the television set. "I'll always love you."

In the morning I looked vulnerable without as well as within. Patrick was scooped up by a birthday party and I sat around the Seneca Room, enjoying my delicate condition. I even had a pencil with me, intending to jot notes on Bizet in the margins of *Vogue.* I wrote "melodically" and then "melody" beneath it, with arrows pointing to it; I still can't figure out what I meant. Louis arrived just before lunch.

"Oh, Sharon," he said. "Oh, God, I'm happy to see you."

I gave him a thrusting smile, hoping he would say how unchanged or unexpectedly lovely or at least how always wonderful I looked, but he said nothing of the sort. He offered me a cigarette, and I had to remind him I'd never smoked — an unnecessary point, and one that started the conversation off badly.

"I thought you smoked," he said. He had to be lying.

"There's no reason for you to remember," I said, wanting to drop it.

"There's every reason for me to remember . . . everything, Sharon."

I waited, but he wasn't in the mood to remember out loud at any rate.

"It's been a long time," we said in chorus.

"Lovely," he said, taking my hand. This was a new item in his repertory; he'd never been much of a handholder before.

"I may be getting married again," he said.

Well, that was that. "Let's have a drink," I said.

"I had to get out of New York. She was pulling a fit in New York."

"Who was?"

"Phyllis. The girl, *you* know. It's been off again, on again.

She's changed. She found out about this other girl and she came into the apartment when Cindy was there. And she threw Cindy's dress down the incinerator. I suppose this sounds like an old story to you."

"So which one are you going to marry?"

"It's a joke to some people, Sharon," he said. "You can't even imagine what people say to me. Our friends. It's as if I were some kind of freak because I've been married three, I mean two times. *That* was a slip." He looked canny, in a way I'd never seen him, and said: "I tell them that the first woman kept trying to kill me and the second woman was made of ice. I say, how can you expect me to marry somebody who doesn't live up to the first two?"

"Our friends?" I said. "Who do you mean?"

"I see Charley and Betsy," he said. "Betsy was telling me the other night that Phyllis needs to suffer. That's her trouble. She doesn't look as if she'd ever suffered anything. I can't talk to her. She just gets mad at me. That's something, of course, when she gets mad."

"Do you and Betsy get along these days?"

He squirmed.

"Louis, which one are you going to marry?"

"Cindy is a sweet kid," he said. "You'd like her." He took my hand again. "Sharon, Betsy says I made a mistake letting you go. She was mad at me for two years because of us."

"But you're all reconciled with Betsy now."

"Yeah." He turned his face to the sun, like a swimmer floating on the bright surface of a pool.

"I don't see Betsy," I said.

"She asks about you. But she understands why you don't write."

"Why don't I write?"

"You were always trying to put the make on Charley,"

Louis said. "Listen, a third marriage is serious, Sharon. I don't want to spend the rest of my life by myself. I'm going to pieces, I really am. I've got a big apartment now and the only loyal friend I have, really and truly, is the maid who comes in and keeps it clean. I've got to have a woman who'll enjoy a nice place, who wants to have babies, all right, babies. Not one of these madwomen." Then he apologized: I wasn't a madwoman, he didn't want me to get mad at him again. Did I remember the time I tore up all his clothes?

"That wasn't me," I said.

"It *was* you. I swear to God it was you. You just don't remember," he said.

"Are you having an affair with Betsy?"

"That's over," he said, indignantly. "That was over a year ago. Just tell me why you let everything go! We had half a chance, you and I. I want to know!" A couple at the bar were frankly staring at us. "Am I embarrassing you?" he asked.

"We were both very stubborn," I said. At that moment, however, I honestly could not remember what we had been like.

"What did you want from me? Jesus Christ, for a while you were even going out with a priest? Don't you know, no marriage is any good but the first one? Susan is my wife — that's who I think of when I think of 'my wife.' I don't know who you are or what you were to me."

"Did you come all the way up here to pick a fight?"

"I didn't expect you'd pretend you don't remember *us*."

"*I* remember!"

"Oh, no, Sharon," he said. "Not the way it was." He had tears in his eyes. "I'll always love you," he said. "Always, always."

"But who will you marry?" I asked.

"I guess I'd better marry Phyllis this time," he said. He

looked at his watch. "I should try to make Boston this evening. There's a conference, I'm giving a paper. I've had an offer from Northeastern, did I tell you? Maybe I'll take it. It's cheaper up there, not such a hassle just surviving. A friend wants me to take over their apartment for a year while she goes to Germany, so I'd have a time to look around. Maybe buy a town house. Leon Watts bought one up there. You can still get maids in Boston. Are you and Dan staying in New York?"

"But I thought you were going to get married."

"I'll get married again," he said. "Why are you so anxious to see me marry again? You and Dan are very lucky, very unusual, you know."

"Oh, no, Louis."

"Let's have lunch. What do you say?" In the dining room he asked a couple of questions about Patrick and then read the menu while I answered; but for the rest of the meal he talked about a textbook he was writing for history of science courses. Only just before he left did the conversation get round again to Phyllis.

"She's threatened to meet me in Boston," he said. "She wants to hear me read this paper. Did I tell you, she finished her M.A.?"

"How would I know that, Louis?"

"No, you wouldn't," he said. "Look at me. Let me look at you."

I looked at him, I stared: but it was like looking at a nice china plate after the meal is over. How nice, I kept thinking, how nice. But then my mind would wander. At a train station you used to wave goodbye and say goodbye and the train would puff and move a fraction of an inch and then not move after all and you had to say goodbye all over again.

"You look wonderful," he said.

"Thank you, Louis."

"Let's get out of here." And we went to the front steps of the hotel. He looked very dapper in his pinch-waisted, double-breasted suit. He had let his sideburns grow. "I want to get you and Dan to dinner one day," he said. He brushed my hair away from my face. "Don't shut me out of your life," he said.

"I'd never do that," I said. "Let me know when you get married."

"Third time's the charm," he said, and then he got into a taxi.

Short Rounds with the Champ

One

Mrs. Damon got a letter from her son's teacher, saying, "He has a discipline problem." Her boy was six years old. Mrs. Damon put the letter away in her jewelry box. "If she wants me to come see her, I will," Mrs. Damon said to herself.

Two

It rained almost every day in March, Mrs. Damon's father broke his hip, and Mr. Damon had to go to Fort Worth three times. At the end of the month Mrs. Damon asked her husband if they could get a divorce. "No," he said. "You haven't thought this thing through. You don't have any grounds for a divorce. How would you like taking care of Chrissie and Bobby all by yourself? We'll drop this subject."

Three

When the roads opened in June Mr. and Mrs. Damon and Chrissie and Bobby drove up into the mountains between Bishop and Lone Pine and camped out one weekend. After lunch on Saturday Mr. Damon nailed a paper plate to a tree and showed Bobby how to shoot a twenty-two pistol. Bobby fired at the paper plate four times without hitting it. "That's the kind of gun they shot Kennedy with," Mrs. Damon said.

"Honey, that was a rifle," Mr. Damon said.

"No, the other Kennedy."

Bobby fired at the paper plate two more times, but he missed it both times.

"That's enough," Mr. Damon said.

"Please, I want to hit it just once," Bobby said.

"Some other time," Mr. Damon said. "Ammunition costs money." He loaded one bullet in the pistol, fired it, and made a hole in the paper plate. "Does your mother want to try it?"

"Mom, do you want to try it?"

"No, you take my turn."

Bobby fired again, but he didn't hit the plate.

"I think you're aiming high," Mr. Damon said.

Four

Mrs. Damon drove Chrissie and Bobby to their grandmother Damon's house in Riverside, and then she drove to

Palm Springs and took a motel room. She bought a bathing suit and had her hair streaked. It was August, and the motel was half closed and almost empty. After her first swim she lay on a lounge chair to dry off. A girl in a brown silk bikini asked her to move to another chair. "That's my chair," the girl said. A little after midnight Mrs. Damon thought she heard somebody trying to get into her room. She got dressed and called Mr. Damon from a payphone in the bar.

"Have a ball," he said. "I don't care when you come back. You come back when you're ready. Who're you with?"

"I'm by myself," she said.

"That's too bad."

When she went home she found a note that said he had gone to Houston for a meeting.

Five

After Chrissie and Bobby were back in school, Mrs. Damon went to her minister and told him her marriage was breaking up. Her minister sent her to a marriage counselor. The marriage counselor asked her to come to a group session and bring Mr. Damon. The marriage counselor and his wife conducted the group session in a duplex in Hollywood. Mrs. Damon saw that the couches came from the Goodwill: the Goodwill had been covering all its upholstered furniture in the same plaid material that summer. There were ashtrays everywhere and a fifty-cup coffee maker. Five other couples came to the session. The oldest couple were Vera and Mike; they had also been to more sessions than anybody else. At the end of the first half hour Mike said to Mr. Damon, "I want you to go over to your wife and tell her that you love her."

"That's hard for me to do," Mr. Damon said.

"I want you to do it," Mike said.

"What are you afraid of?" Vera asked.

"What am I afraid of, honey?" Mr. Damon asked his wife. To Vera he said, "I'm not that way. It isn't my way to say what I feel."

"What do you feel?" Mike asked. "Do you love her? If you love her, tell her that."

Mr. Damon went over to Mrs. Damon and kissed her. "I love you, honey," he said.

Later in the session Mrs. Damon asked everybody, "What should I do?"

"Grow up," Vera said. "You aren't a child any more."

Mr. and Mrs. Damon didn't go back to see the marriage counselor; they didn't go to another group session.

"I'm not getting anything out of it," Mr. Damon said.

Six

Mrs. Damon fell in love with the man who taught ceramics and firing at the recreation center. For several weeks they had coffee together after class and told each other about their childhood and all the people they had been in love with. When he told her about his first wife's abortion, she told him that she once wanted to divorce her husband, and the next time Mr. Damon went out of town the man came to the house after dark and stayed all night in her room. That night she said she didn't want to have sex with him, but they went ahead anyway.

"I don't want the kids to hear," Mrs. Damon said.

"They know I'm here."

"No they don't," she said.

After that Mrs. Damon sometimes made the children take

sleeping pills, and on those nights she built a fire in the fire-place. She and her boyfriend lay on the rug in front of the fire and drank wine. She was very happy.

Seven

Mr. and Mrs. Damon went to a PTA meeting to hear arguments about sex education in the schools. Just before the meeting started a teacher approached them and said that she wanted to talk to them about Bobby's discipline problem. Mr. Damon laughed and said, "You're the one that has the discipline problem. I don't have any discipline problem with him."

During the meeting a gray-haired man stood up and said, "Let's not fool ourselves. These kids know everything there is to know about sex. They know more than I know about sex. The way these girlies dress these days, they know what they're showing off. I want to make sure they don't spread the clap. If you want to know the truth I'm worried my kids are going to get the clap from one of these little whores." Several people shouted at the man to sit down and shut up. Mr. Damon walked up to the man and said, "Shut your filthy mouth." Then he punched him. The blow fell a little short. The gray-haired man burst into tears and swung first one fist and then the other, but neither touched Mr. Damon. He and Mr. Damon kept trying, and both men had to be restrained physically. The gray-haired man then said he would make a formal complaint to the police. "Do that," Mr. Damon said.

Eight

In May Mr. and Mrs. Damon decided to buy a camper, for family vacations. On Sunday afternoons they went to sales lots together and looked at new models. During the week Mrs. Damon answered newspaper ads inserted by owners who wanted to sell. One afternoon she drove all the way out to a house in Chatsworth to look at a Traveleze. Nobody was home but the owner, a middle-aged man with a scar from his hairline to his jaw, who said he was retired. "Even my dog's gone shopping," the man said. He would say something and then stop and look hard into her eyes until she said something back.

"What kind of a dog?" she asked him.

He would also pause a long time before he answered, looking hard into her eyes again.

After a while he said, "A German shepherd."

"Lots of people are afraid of those," she said.

After a while he said, "Yes they are." And then he said, "Nobody who gets to know Dusty is afraid of him. Nobody will be hurt by Dusty."

She couldn't think what to say next.

"Do you know something?" he said. "You have got the face of a little girl, but you have the eyes of a mature woman. Do you know what I'm talking about?"

"No," she said.

"I think you know what I'm talking about," he said.

"No I don't," she said.

"You can have it your way," he said.

Mrs. Damon said she wanted to look at the Traveleze, and he led her around the house to the driveway, where the

Traveleze was parked in front of an old black Cadillac. The Traveleze was in very bad condition; there were hundreds of little scars and scratches, cigarette burns and dents and nicks all over the interior.

"It's been lived in," the owner said.

"It needs a lot of work, I guess," she said.

After a while he said, "You don't have to buy it," as if all along she had thought she had to.

"Come back and see us," he said. "Come back soon."

"We'll see," Mrs. Damon said.

Nine

Mrs. Damon and her boyfriend were lying in front of the fireplace, and her boyfriend said, "I wonder if I would be in love with you if I wasn't afraid of your husband. I wonder if I would come here."

Mrs. Damon replied, "I guess you wouldn't."

Ten

Mr. and Mrs. Damon and Chrissie and Bobby went on a vacation trip in their new camper. Mr. Damon taught Bobby how to cast with a real fishing rod. Mrs. Damon showed Chrissie how to pan for gold with an aluminum pie plate. At night the children slept in the camper and Mr. and Mrs. Damon slept in a tent beside it.

Mr. Damon told his wife that he wanted to try new ways of making love.

"Where did you get that idea?" she asked him.

"I read a book," he said. "Don't *resist* me."

"I don't want to resist you."

"Don't be scared. This is a perfectly natural thing. Anything is natural and good as long as you enjoy it."

Later she said, "I don't enjoy it."

Mr. Damon got angry.

"I enjoy it," he said. "Why can't you enjoy it? Relax and enjoy it. I can't enjoy it if you don't."

Eleven

When they got back home after their vacation in the mountains, Mr. Damon told Mrs. Damon that he took part in an orgy on a plane to Atlanta one night. The stewardess played with him and one of the co-pilots at the same time. There was nobody else on the plane except the crew and a couple of soldiers sleeping in tourist.

"You're crazy," Mrs. Damon said. "That never happened to you."

"It happens all the time," Mr. Damon said. "Do you like that story?"

"What do you mean?"

"Would you do that if you were a stewardess?"

"It never happened to you," Mrs. Damon said.

Twelve

Mrs. Damon woke up one morning at ten to six. When she looked at the clock on the night table and saw that the alarm was up and set for seven, she couldn't figure out what had awakened her. Finally she looked up and saw Bobby standing near the door. He was aiming his father's twenty-two pistol at her. "Put that down," she said. "You must not play with that pistol."

Mr. Damon woke up. When he saw Bobby with the pistol he said, "I'm gonna have to insist you put that gun down, fellow. That's against the rules, fellow."

Bobby said, "Ha ha, it is *not* against the rules."

He fired the pistol and the bullet missed Mr. Damon by less than two inches. It made a little hole and a stink in the moulding of the headboard.

Brief Lives, from Next Door

When Ida and Marion lived next to us, my mother took her side and my father took his. Naturally enough. My father, who did not drink or gamble or chase women, said, "Marion's a good-natured guy. He's just got a temper, that's all, and not much sense. He likes his snort once in a while, so he likes to think he's a hell of a fellow." And my mother said, "Ida's the long-suffering type. She'll put up with anything, year after year. She never thinks of herself. But she has the boy to think about." In the afternoons my mother went over to Ida's house and told her to get a divorce and a big fat alimony settlement from Marion. "He can have all the little gal friends he wants to on what's left over," my mother would say, and finish with "ha-ha-ha-*ha!*" Ida, who had a small, drooping, pear-shaped face, looked unaroused. If this had been a horse-race, she'd have been running at fifty-to-one. Yet, a few years later Ida got in the Rambler and drove to Redwood City and got a divorce from Marion; then she took her son, Tim, and moved into an apartment house in Sunnyvale and supported that establishment by working in the post office. "That was the smartest move you ever made, Ida," my mother used to say. Ida neither agreed nor disagreed. Marion had fled the state rather than pay alimony. Ten years later something went wrong with Ida's kidneys and she died. Last Sunday my father looked around to make sure my mother was in the kitchen and then said he'd been down to Pismo Beach to visit Marion.

"In Pismo Beach?"

"He's got some kind of part-time job as a landscape gardener," my father said enviously. "He doesn't know anything about landscape gardening. But he makes a living, between that and his social security."

Whenever I saw Marion I thought: *That's what my mother thought was a handsome man.* He was big and big-boned — heavier than is fashionable now — he had a little Don Ameche moustache, and he wore soft plaid wool shirts, expensive thin wool trousers. Sometimes he was a salesman and sometimes he was a publicity man, but he was always a heavy drinker and a promiscuous lover, or so I gathered from my mother's comments when she peeped through the venetian blinds in our dining room and watched Marion's car — a Plymouth coupe, painted dull green like a school radiator — spurt away toward the city. I never said anything one way or another, but I agreed with my father that Ida was nothing to stay home for. Yet who of us knew Ida? We knew only my mother's voice, coming from Ida as from a ventriloquist's dummy:

"Ida says she gave Marion every chance, every chance in the world," my mother said. "Then one day, she said, she put her foot down and told Marion he was going to do right by

Tim even if he didn't do right by her. We-ell, you could have knocked our Marion over with a feather, she said. He should have known she wouldn't put up with that forever."

Then my mother took a long, deep breath and stared at my father. My father picked his teeth and hummed. This went on for ten years.

"The minute that Marion tries to come back to California they'll have him in jail!" my mother cried happily. Then Ida's kidneys went wrong and Marion came back to California, driving a Mustang, getting his social security checks care of general delivery, Anywhere, California.

"Marion is in Monterey," my father wrote a year ago. "He says he's the public relations man for an Italian restaurant. He doesn't know a darned thing about the restaurant business."

I saw Ida once about a year before she died. She liked her job at the post office. "There's what I'd call a personality conflict with that other supervisor," my mother added, but Ida looked neither here nor there. "A government job gives you real security," my mother said. Ida wore knit ensembles and preferred real jewelry, no matter how small and unpleasant-looking. "It's made all the difference to you to get a job, hasn't it, Ida?" my mother said, and Ida, smiling, showed off her real teeth — small and faintly golden. She had the rather stupid look of a woman who listens to her insides and knows what's going on; in any event she seemed to know about her kidneys some time before the doctors did, because she got everything in order a month after I last saw her and went back to her home town in South Dakota to spend her vacation. While she was there she wrote a letter to my mother, and I stole the letter because I was fascinated to hear, at last, Ida's real voice:

> It is as beautiful here as I remember it, this is a bless-
> ing as I was honestly scared to go home. Oh there are sad
> things. My aunt (84) in a nursing home. Family house
> gone, etc. Everything a little small and rundown after
> California. But am reminded every day of something I
> thought was forgotten for ever. Had coffee with the
> Dale Springers (Mother's cousin's boy and his wife)
> and we surely laughed a lot at nothing. I guess they'd
> lock us up if they saw us laughing at nothing like that.
> Tim has made some new friends for which I thank
> God. He was surely a help on the driving and I count
> on him at all times now.

Tim is exactly my age. He is tall, like his father, but he
has all his mother's undistinguished features, including her
small golden teeth. When we were children I didn't like to
play with him because he was too fussy about his toys. My
sister and I used to go into his room, a luxurious place in
our estimation: Tim — an only child — had not only a room
all his own but his own door that opened into the back yard.
Distracted by his toys and books, particularly by a pumpkin-
colored children's encyclopedia full of craft projects, we ig-
nored Tim. "Did you ever make this?" Carol asked, showing
him the diagram for a homemade parachute. "No, I never
made it," he said angrily. "Those are my books."

"You don't make any of the stuff in your books." Carol
and I hated waste. Carol made dolls out of the old faucets
she found in the basement. I rooted in the neighborhood
trash cans and found beaded purses and discarded copies of
The Woman's Home Companion. We wanted to make rugs
out of my mother's old nylons, but my mother said this was
disgusting. "Please lend me your books," Carol said to Tim.

"You can't have my books. I don't want you to look at

them." He pulled the books out of our hands and put them
in his toy chest.

"Marion had a swell house for himself right around here.
Then he got rid of it. Oh, gee, is he sick about that," my
father said.

"Why did he get rid of it?"

"Oh, well, it's not a very happy story. He wanted Tim
to live with him and he did for a while and then he left and
Marion got mad and sold the house."

"Why?"

"I don't know," my father said, fearfully.

How old my parents were, now. At some time — a few
years before — they had acknowledged that they needed
us, they had gotten together in the night perhaps and agreed
on it, perhaps. Or perhaps they had done no such thing —
rather, Carol and I had agreed that now they needed us.
However difficult, incomprehensible, incompetent, slovenly
we were. It went one way, then another. I had taken care of
the baby for two months and now I needed my father.

"I don't know why Tim left," my father had said, fearfully. When we drove back to Millbrae it was dark. Pale
white clouds hung from the black sky. My father was sleeping. I considered my memory of a photograph I'd once
seen of my parents and Ida and Marion sitting at the same
table at a dinner party in Hillsborough, just before the war.
Their clothes, their bodies, even the cloth on the table looked
heavy and well made. Marion has his right elbow on the
table, his left hand on Ida's shoulder; his moustache is quite
black, and his eyes are black too. My mother's eyes are closed;
she's smoking a cigarette. My father's eyes are closed, but he's
smiling with his mouth open — he must have just said, "Go
ahead! Take the picture." Behind them the French doors look

out on darkness. Beyond the frame of the picture there is a piano where somebody is playing "Avalon." While my mother and Ida dance with other men, Marion tells my father about a fellow who just came back from Hong Kong on the China Clipper. "I'd like to know exactly what those Japs want," says Marion, working himself up for a trip to Japan. Representing a company, selling airplane parts . . .

"He wanted Tim to live with him in that house," my father says.

A year after Ida died, Marion bought a tiny house in Redwood City and asked Tim to come live with him. Marion even bought two cars, secondhand but clean and well-tuned. He bought a color television set and lawn furniture. He bought a screen and projector for his color slides. Tim worked in the Greyhound office and wanted to save money.

But after Marion had lived with Tim for a while, he realized that he didn't like him very much. "Everything he says is full of that goddamn irony," my father reported. "He can't say anything straight out, that's what Marion says. Finally Marion says to him, 'Just tell me what you want to say. I'm not smart enough for this ironic stuff.' " Tim also claimed to be a fervent Christian, and when he wasn't being ironic he would keep his father sitting up until well after midnight to talk about miracles and what was the truth about prayer cures. Malarkey, said Marion.

Yet — or so my father claimed — Marion bitterly regretted his haste in getting rid of the house. He could have lived there alone. He likes to work with his hands. He has an apartment now, in San Luis Obispo, but he writes to my father to complain that the apartment is too small and the other apartments are all occupied by old, deaf people who nevertheless complain about the noise of Marion's radio.

"Marion's sixty-nine himself, but he hasn't cut out the booze or cigarettes," says my father, enviously.

"Daddy," I say. "We'll never leave you."

"It's too late now," he says, and he laughs.

Any day now he expects Marion to move somewhere else, and buy another house, and settle down.

When You Go Away

Just before they left they got a card from Susan and Willie: "Come to us! We won't forgive you if you pass us by!"

"What can we take them?" Charlotte asked, putting the card in her purse, an enormous pocketbook supplied like a small country: there were maps, letters, medicines, cosmetics, film, cookies in cellophane, raisins in boxes, small articles of clothing and paper handkerchiefs. "What about a cake from Mrs. Rockne?"

"I thought Susan's boy might like that bow," Charlotte's husband said. He had a woodworking shed and the car was full of his presents: salad bowls, cigarette boxes, pencil holders, yo-yo's, bows and arrows. He liked to make these things to give away, but he could not himself take pride in them: Charlotte had to have a cake or some flowers to go along. Yet, his works were lovely. The wood of the salad bowls was as smooth as sunlight on an old pond, the bows as supple as new saplings.

When they drove away from the house the neighbor's cow

looked up and her calf danced. Thunderheads were way down the green-bordered road ahead of them.

"Oh, Lord, look at that!" Charlotte said. "Will we have a good storm?"

"I don't know, I do not," Rube said. "We don't care, either."

They drove and picnicked, neatly, in the roadside rests, and drove some more. That night they shared a double bed in a motel outside Columbus. "That's a good program," Charlotte said to the television. "Rube, I wish we got that program at home." He was asleep. She gazed on him as kindly as the moon. "Take care of them all," she said, her nightly prayer. She got up gently and wrote a postcard to Ella Lockridge, who had just lost Ed.

The next morning Charlotte was still talking about that program. "I don't agree with that fellow's ideas, Rube," she said. "But he got to Bill Buckley once in a while. I could see it. It was worth listening to."

Rube listened, but he had nothing to say in reply. "Finish your breakfast, Mother. Let's get on the road."

"You can't sit still, can you?" she said and smiled. She also smiled at the waitress and the cashier. In the parking lot she said, "Rube, where are my sunglasses?"

"On your head," he said.

That afternoon he said, at a roadside stop, "Well, now we got to decide. About Susan and Willie."

"I feel the same way," she said. They both looked grim with their sunglasses over their eyes. "I have that cake, of course."

"About thirty miles," he said. "No need to stay."

"We'll be tired," she said. "Won't we, Dad?"

Two old people in their car together. The shadows of the trees were as long as rivers. In a scrap of sunlight on the scuffed grass stood a broken plastic thermos jug, bright orange.

"Excuse me," Charlotte said. She got out of the car and picked up the thermos, and then some hot dog wrappings, and threw them in the trash can. She looked around, as she might look around her living room. Theirs was the only car remaining.

"All right," she said to Rube.

When Rube stopped the car in Willie's country driveway, Charlotte said, "We should have called."

"Are they home?"

The garage door was shut. The front door of the house was shut. No porch light was on; the living room window was dark.

"Dark," Charlotte said. "All that way."

Rube got out of the car and went to ring the bell; at that distance his face looked unfamiliar and pale.

"I can't hear you!" Charlotte said. "Let's go!"

Then the door opened. Rube was talking to somebody, yet no light was turned on.

"Rube," Charlotte said, getting out of the car.

Susan's boy was standing just inside the door. He was eleven or twelve, about five feet tall, and he had thin brown hair. He was wearing a plaid cotton sports coat and a white shirt and a green bow tie and green trousers. His shoes were shined. "Who are you?" he asked.

"You know who we are," Charlotte said. "What a joke." She looked past him but she couldn't see any lights.

"I don't know who you are," the boy said. His eyes kept moving and moving.

"You know who we are, I told you," Rube said. His head

began to shake. "Let's write a finish to the joke. Let us in, now."

The boy was looking past them; then looked at them again. "Tell me who you are," he said.

Charlotte said, "Where are your Mom and Dad?"

"They're here," the boy said. He tried to close the door, but Rube leaned against it to hold it open.

"Just a minute, young fellow," Rube said. "Don't you close that door on us."

The boy threw himself on the door and shut it, knocking Rube backwards; Rube fell to his knees on the porch, and Charlotte burst into tears. "He hurt you," she said. "I know he hurt you."

"No, no," Rube said. "I'm all right."

"No, I know he hurt you. Oh, Rube, I can't stand this." Her skin had turned gray-green, like a stone. "Where are you hurt?" she asked in a weak and expressionless voice. "Tell me."

He put his arms around her and made her sit down on the steps. After a minute the crickets started up in the grass. Mosquitoes sang around their ears. He rubbed her shoulders, first with one hand, then with the other. "Will you get me my purse?" she asked at last. When he brought it to her she took out a heart-shaped bottle of smelling salts and a paper handkerchief. "I don't want to be sick here," she said.

"Mother, are you going to be sick?"

"I don't want to be sick here," she said. The stench of ammonia curled through the air.

Rube turned to the door and pounded on it. "Open the door!" he said. "You open the door, now, do you hear me." But there was no sound. Then he saw that the boy was standing in the living room window, watching them, as still as a hat rack. Rube went to the window and the boy took a single step backwards.

"Open the door," Rube yelled. "She's sick."

The boy turned his head toward Charlotte, who was wiping her forehead with a tissue, who looked at them both with unfocused eyes. "Where is Susan?" she asked. "Where are they? Where are Susan and Willie?"

Rube picked up a rock and threw it at the window; they could hear the boy call out, the pane of glass fall. The boy darted out of sight. Rube ran slowly around the corner of the house.

"Don't run!" Charlotte said.

The boy opened the front door. "Tell him to go away," the boy said. "You have to go away. Leave us alone."

"Where's your mother?"

"You can't talk to them. I won't let you," the boy said.

There were noises from the back of the house.

"He'll get in the back door," Charlotte said.

"Oh, no!" the boy screamed. He slammed the door.

The only other house Charlotte could see was across the road, and there was a realtor's sign in front of it. To her left the sky was deep blue and half a moon hung in the middle of the heavens. To her right there were big clouds and red light from the setting sun. The door behind Charlotte opened at last and the boy walked past her, down the steps, and lay down in the grass and closed his eyes. He crossed his hands on his breast.

"They're in the den," Rube said, coming out on the steps too. "Aren't you cold?"

"My hands," Charlotte said. She got up little by little with Rube's assistance and followed him through the house to a door with a crack of light beneath it. An artificial voice came up from the basement. Rube opened the door and the voice said: ". . . highlights, we must include Palmer's birdie on the fifteenth."

They followed the artificial voice downstairs to another door and opened it. Willie was still sitting in his reclining chair, but Susan was on her feet, gathering the remains of their tray supper: aluminum serving dishes, plastic glasses and lots of paper napkins.

"That was the funniest thing," Susan said. "I thought we could hear the doorbell down here. Why, I've *heard* the doorbell down here. I guess you could have pounded on the door all night and we'd never have heard you."

"All night," Willie said, glumly. He'd turned off the television's sound but still looked at the picture. His face and neck were claret red.

"Let's have a drink," Susan said. "What'll it be."

There was a thump-thump-thump on the stairs and the boy came into the room.

"Didn't you hear Rube and Charlotte?" his mother asked.

"No," the boy said.

"Well say hello now," Susan said. "Go on."

"Hello, Mr. Bird," the boy said. "Mrs. Bird." He shook hands with them in turn, with no more expression than a cat.

"Hello, Robbie," Charlotte said.

Then he tried to take her hand again and squeeze her fingers, but she pulled it away just in time.

"You're just in time for dessert," Susan said. "And you'll stay tonight."

Finally Rube said, "We have reservations."

"Oh," Susan said. She sneered. "Don't like us, huh?" Then she smiled. "You *two!*" she said. "You *two.*"

After chocolate cake and coffee and brandy Willie kept Rube in the dining room to tell him about selling office equipment.

"I was almost a doctor, you know that, Rube?" Willie asked. "That's why I like my work, you see? What do you notice? Anything different?" Willie leaned forward in his chair and Rube leaned forward in his, as if they were about to kiss. "See it?"

"I don't know, Willie," Rube said.

"I'm a hippie now. Get it?"

"Who?"

"Aw, the hell with it!" Willie bounced back in his chair as if he had been punched in the face. "The hell with it! I say the kids are right! It's not worth it. Rube. *In a pig's eye it's not worth it!*" He got up and opened a cabinet and took out a shiny black cardboard box. "I want to show you something, Rube. You're interested in woodworking. I know that. You'll get a kick out of this."

In the black cardboard box, in a nest of white tissue paper, there was a glass bowl engraved with a wild horse running across a prairie.

"Hand carved," Willie said. "What do you think of that, Rube?"

"May I pick it up?"

"You sure as hell can," Willie said. "That cost me more than I care to say."

"Thank you," Rube said.

"I'll tell you the secret, what I was going to say. I'm growing a moustache."

"I didn't notice."

"You didn't notice. You did-n't no-tice. Let me tell you, Rube, we've got to start noticing. Taking a little notice, huh?"

And Susan and Charlotte were up in Susan's bedroom, where Susan had unbuttoned her blouse and was lying on the bed, fanning herself with a magazine. "If we could air condition the whole house, hm? Wouldn't that be something?"

"My arthritis," Charlotte said.

"I know," Susan said. "But you look just wonderful, Charlotte. You do. Your skin is as soft as a baby's. You'll probably tell me it's just soap and cold water or no soap at all. I was in Wanamaker's the other day and this old biddy tried to sell me a truckload of stuff and I told her that the gal with the nicest complexion I knew never used anything but soap and cold water. You should have seen her splutter!"

"Robbie's grown," Charlotte said.

"Thank you," Susan said. "We haven't had a minute's worry out of him. But it won't last. In a couple of years he'll be shooting marijuana in himself and everything else and his hair will be down to his butt. I know it and I even say, Good for him! You won't understand but I say, Good for him! This is some crummy old world those young people are getting handed. They're not getting it on a silver platter. We're grateful for what we've had."

"He's quiet," Charlotte said.

"How are your grandchildren?" Susan asked.

"Just fine," Charlotte said.

"Well don't you have any pictures, heaven's sakes?"

"I don't carry them," Charlotte said. "Susan, dear, I'm as tired as tired can be. I'm going to collect Rube and make him take us on to the motel."

"I wish I knew why you won't stay here," Susan said, with a sly look as she buttoned her blouse again.

When they went out in the hall Robbie was standing in the door of the bathroom in his skivvies. "Are you leaving?" he asked.

"Why don't you just throw them out?" his mother asked.

"No," Robbie said.

"We have to go," Charlotte said.

Robbie sighed loudly. "Goodbye," he said.

"That's my honey," Susan said to Robbie and she gave his shoulders a squeeze.

"Goodbye, Robbie," Charlotte said.

When they were all gathered again on the doorstep, the gnats were dancing in the porchlight and the moon was now in the other side of the sky, Willie asked Susan where Robbie was. "Upstairs," she said. "He said goodbye."

"Tell that little son of a gun to get down here," Willie said. Then he laughed.

"That's all right," Charlotte said.

Charlotte kissed Willie and Susan. Susan kissed Rube and Charlotte. There were no lights to be seen in any direction. Then they started the car, turned on the lights and backed down the driveway, Charlotte waving goodbye and goodbye and goodbye.

"Just the same," Charlotte said, when they were on the highway again.

"He was a nice little fellow when he was about three or four," Rube said. "When I had my tools in the back of the garage, he used to come in and watch me. I made him a wagon."

"No, that was for Mark," Charlotte said.

"Was it? I thought it was for him. It doesn't matter. He wouldn't remember," Rube said.

A Line of Order

And over all this chaos of history and legend, of fact
and supposition, he strove to draw out a line of
order, to reduce the abysses of the past to order by
a diagram.
— *Stephen Hero*

There is a compulsion worse than nostalgia: to return to a
scene of past unhappiness, as if one expected it to turn out
right — this time! When I went back to Sand River my cousins were there, and their own lives trailed around them like
unfinished quilts. But to my surprise Saint Agnes' School was
gone, torn down, all its possibilities lost. Once I read several
books about nuns and convent schools; they were nothing
like Saint Agnes'. Now Saint Agnes' School disappears. Its
grounds are rubble, weeds, rubble. I walked back and forth
across the leveled block, but the rubble was beaten so small
that not even one whole brick was left.

"The sisters don't look like sisters anymore," my cousin
Joan said.

They dress, I am told, in dowdy blue and black, utility
sheers, stout shoes, hats of an old-fashioned military cut.
There's a car pool to Gleeson High School, where there are
young, Tiparillo-smoking, joking priests to teach the boys and
girls (strictly a day school). The mothers, I gather, are worried that their children will marry Negroes. "I've talked to the
Negro people," says Father Larry Shuler, "and they want to
marry their own."

Not a board, not a brick. I can convince nobody, scarcely myself, that Saint Agnes' School was once an establishment of substance in a wealthy district. (There are signs now in the fat windows of those wide, veranda-skirted houses: ROOMS). I never saw the district in that heyday, of course, but my mother did.

I walked back and forth across the rubble, looking for Saint Agnes' lamb, a stone lamb, painted white; it used to stand in a niche over the front door of the school, over the arc of stone letters — *Saint Agnes' School*.

My father came back from the Pacific when the war was finished and asked for a divorce. My mother gave it to him. We had been living with her parents on a little farm in Wilson, almost fifty miles from Sand River, and I'd been happy there. I was ready to start school with Bobby Lyons and Norma Mary Metz: already, that summer, we had begun to study the yard of the local public school — the Warshaw School. My grandmother would walk us there in the evenings and sit on a bench near the teeter-totter while we tried the swings. The Warshaw School had an enormous black metal fire slide — we called it a fire escape, but it was in fact an enormous iron tube that went at an angle from the second floor down to the ground. In case of fire, my grandmother said, children could be thrown into the tube, by which they'd slide to safety. Bobby Lyons climbed into the lower mouth of the fire slide and shouted and pounded. "I can't wait to go down that old thing," he said.

"I hope there's a fire," Norma Mary said boldly.

"There won't be any fire," my grandmother said. We had to agree with her, for the Warshaw School was built all of brick, the only brick building in town besides the Methodist church, and it stood upon a wide field of asphalt. My grandmother led us home in the near dark; heat lightning licked across the sky at the end of Fourth Street. "The lightning'll catch the school on fire someday I bet," Bobby Lyons said.

"It will not," my grandmother said. "But they'll have a fire drill one day and you'll get to go down the fire slide." And then changing her mind: "Oh, I hope they don't. It must be nasty filthy dirty in that old pipe."

"Fire drill!" Bobby Lyons yelled, running ahead, sliding on the pebbles on the summer-beaten road. "Fire drill!"

But my mother realized that she would have to go to Sand River to find a new husband, and I would go to Sand River and board at Saint Agnes' School, which had been one of the finest Catholic schools in the Rocky Mountains (my mother said). The sisters taught good manners (my grandmother said). "I was a damn fool to marry outside the Church!" my mother said to my grandmother: they agreed it had been an unlucky thing to do. My grandmother had gone to Saint Agnes' School, and she remembered with pleasure the school parties and processions. Once she had walked from Saint Agnes' School to Saint Michael's Cathedral, a mile along Bannock Street, wearing a white gown and roses wreathed upon her head: a handmaiden of the Blessed Virgin. The daughters of silver millionaires had gone to the school in those days, and French and Irish priests came from San Francisco to give lectures on moral theology and literature —

— these things I know now, but then I listened to my mother and my grandmother and thought of: velvet, silver, roses. My grandmother in her petticoat. French — which for some reason meant "clean" to me; perhaps there was a French laundry in Sand River. I thought of Christmas: when I went to Saint Agnes' School, I decided, it would be like Christmas morning. There would be candles and carols, and everything would be new. My mother drove to Sand River one weekend and came back with new clothes: white cotton undershirts, brown stockings and garter belts, white blouses, two navy blue smocks, and a navy blue sailor coat with four brass buttons and a navy insignia, embroidered with scarlet thread, on the left sleeve.

In September, twenty-five years ago, it was a hundred degrees at noon, and by ten o'clock in the morning the hot light was already beginning to penetrate the vault of poplar leaves that hung over my grandparents' yard. In one corner of the yard there was a concrete well of sorts, a little box that poured water into a ditch no wider than my body, and I followed my grandfather to this well, where he opened the gate, and then followed him along the ditch as he made cuts with a shovel to let the water flood the lawn. The water was cold at first, and I was afraid of the earthworms his shovel revealed, but soon the lawn was covered with an inch of water; I ran back and forth across the shallow lake, kicking up plumes of water and watching the drops form in the air before they fell again. A shift of the wind brought the smell of alfalfa from the field behind us; from my enormous grotto I could see the sun-dazzled field and a man on a tractor cutting the alfalfa.

At noon my grandfather banked the ditch again, and the water soaked down under the grass, and my footsteps were erased as the blades sprang back. Norma Mary Metz came walking down the glaring dirt street and I met her at the corner. She had sweat on her face.

"Are you through with school?" I asked.

"I have to go back after lunch. I can't talk to you. I just have an hour to eat lunch, and I want to go back and play with Carol. I'm going to get my mama to fix me a lunch in a lunch-box. The school food is icky. Why aren't you in school? You're supposed to be in school."

"You cried the first day," I said.

"I didn't."

I said, "I saw you when your mother brought you back."

"Wayne Harrison pulled my braids," she said.

"I'm going to school tomorrow."

"Then I can wait for you and we'll walk together."

"No, you can't. I'm going to a boarding school in Sand River."

"I just thought bad kids went to boarding schools," she said. "What did you do?"

"I didn't do anything, it's not for bad kids."

Later, when it was time for Norma Mary and Bobby Lyons to come back from school, I hid in the woodshed.

Then it began to storm. My mother and grandmother came hurrying down the street with packages in their hands, shouting for my grandfather and me to get the chairs in off the lawn, while behind them thunderheads reared over the trees, showing their black bellies, and the wind started lifting the branches of the poplars. When we got inside the back porch I could hear the trees very loudly. All summer they roared in the sunshine, but in a storm it was as if waves were breaking over us, and I could hear soughs and creaks and cracks. Then my grandmother told me to keep off the back porch, for she was afraid that a limb would break and fall through that flimsy roof. Then the rain came, tearing the leaves from their twigs, and my grandfather ran to the woodshed and brought back a bucket of coal and a bucket of kindling, while my grandmother stood at the back door, holding her flying hair away from her face.

After dinner my grandfather went to sleep in his chair next to the radio, and all I could hear were the railroad clock and the rain and women's voices from the bedroom. I went out to the sleeping porch, where the canvas over the screens was bulging in the wind. My grandmother kept the victrola in there. I cranked it up and put on a record:

> *He's got*
> *Curly hair*
> *I never cared for*
> *Curly hair*
> *But he's got*
> *Curly hair*
> *And that's my weakness now.*

I watched myself tap-dancing, barefoot, in the wardrobe mirror.

My Uncle Dwight drove us to Sand River the next afternoon, and by the time we arrived, it was almost dark. "Just go out on Bannock," my mother said. She rolled down her window; the green, aromatic smell of elm-spray filled the car. The streets were lined with enormous elms, with big houses sunk in ample gardens. "Here we are," my mother said. Uncle Dwight stopped in front of a four story Victorian building, constructed of brick and ornamented with ironwork, standing by itself as proprietor of a whole block. The building, in its turn, was dominated by its bell tower, which began as a porch for the door, continued up the front of the building, and then rose alone into the sky, lifting a gold cross above the elms to the last ray of sunlight.

My mother led me up the walk while Uncle Dwight followed with my suitcase and my blue tin trunk; but after setting the trunk down in the hall he shot back to the car. The floors and Edwardian woodwork beamed with polish; a hemp runner, very narrow, showed where one might walk: either straight ahead to the end of the hall where a niche held a large statue of Our Lady of the Immaculate Conception, or to the right and up a broad staircase. Midway down the corridor a door opened and a tall, heavy nun came forward to greet us, her face as immobile as the moon in a halo of starched linen. "Hello," she said, "I'm Sister Mary Stephen." Abruptly my mother caught me and kissed me again and pointed out my trunk to Sister Stephen, and Sister Stephen assured my mother in a hearty voice that I would have a wonderful time. "There's a little girl waiting for you," Sister Stephen said. "Her name is Patsy and she wants to know when you arrive." Impatient now, I gave my mother a last kiss and watched her go out the front door. The front door closed. I followed Sister Stephen up the stairs.

She led me into a dormitory on the second floor: white walls, white ceiling, white iron beds, white dressers, white curtains, and ten little girls in white nightgowns that hung to their ankles. When she put my suitcase on the bed and opened it, I found that it smelled of freshly washed nightgowns too, and soap. Sister Stephen told me to undress under my nightgown; all the other girls, briefly informed of my name, were doing the same thing, and they looked like moths struggling in cocoons while Sister Stephen moved among them, undoing braids and unbuttoning dresses.

Patsy had coppery hair in a single long braid down her back; she was not allowed to speak to me, but as a gesture of welcome she reached down, grabbed the hem of her nightgown, and pulled it up, revealing a round little bare body. There was a rush of giggles, like raindrops blown against a window, and then silence. Sister Stephen explained that we were about to go to the bathroom, that we would do what we had to do, then wash our hands and faces and brush our teeth; we must not talk or make noise, and we must not drink any water, because this would mean we'd have to get up in the night. Standing in my robe and slippers, holding my towel and washcloth and toothpaste and toothbrush and cup, I was afraid of the whiteness and silence. I saw Sister Stephen pinch the arm of a girl who was dawdling.

I was given a place in the procession to the bathroom, and once there I was careful not to swallow a drop of water. When we returned, Sister Stephen told us to kneel, and with our noses in the sides of our long-legged beds, we prayed in unison to Mary and then to our guardian angel:

> *Angel of God, my guardian dear*
> *To whom God's love entrusts me here,*
> *Ever this day be at my side*
> *To light and guard, to rule and guide.*
> *Amen.*

A scene from the dormitory: I am lying on my bed, repeating the alphabet to myself (I have just learned it), trying out different rhythmic groupings of the letters, settling finally on the syncopated ABCD EFG HIJK LMNOP — QRS TUV Double-youuuuuu X YZ.

A scene from the classroom: Sister Stephen, in the yellow light of a dark afternoon, is printing the words *hat, bat, cat* on the board, and I am reading them and savoring the shape of the vowel in my mouth, trying to remember other words for the list. I liked the classroom. I was neither quick enough to be bored nor slow enough to fall behind. The rules of grammar, punctuation and penmanship protected me: I could understand them. Two years before I had made a game of writing the letters of the alphabet, which I could write but not read, in any order at all on sheets of paper. When I cov-

ered a sheet I took it to my mother and asked her if I had
written any words. Now, at six, I had real words to write as
I wished, and with a big yellow pencil I made the shapes of
printed small letters, each of which had assumed a character: dwarfish *a*'s, submarine *p*'s, talkative *e*'s, and *d*, who I
thought was like the joker in a pack of cards.

A scene from Sunday: I am standing in the parlor, listening to my mother, but I cannot look at her. She asks me, "Are
you having a good time here?" — or something like that, perhaps, "I'll bet you're having a good time here, aren't you?"
I say yes because that is the right thing to say. In a few weeks
I have learned that I must always do the right thing. At
breakfast time that Sunday Sister Stephen had led us, as
usual, to the long breakfast table in the basement. The table
frightened me in the early morning: it was crowded with
cheap, heavy china, nickel-plated knives, forks and spoons,
pots, jugs — and the low ceiling was covered with pipes
bending this way and that like the gnarled roots of a tree:
as if we were eating deep underground, under the tree. The
steam hissed and gurgled above us. I no longer wanted to eat
breakfast, because every morning the moment came when I
had to pick up my cup, break the film with my lip, and drink
down the chocolate that was tepid, thick and very sweet. At
first I had said, "Please, I don't want to drink it." Sister Stephen insisted. I refused. She commanded. I drank it and at
once threw up. "That's nasty! That's disgusting!" she cried,
and my punishment was to stay in the basement for an hour
after the others had left.

"Do you like Sister Mary Stephen?" my mother asks.
"Yes, I like her a lot," I say.
After a while one of the sisters comes into the parlor, and
this is the signal that visiting hours are over; it is suppertime.

When my mother leaves I remember that I was going to ask her if I were an orphan. One of the day pupils told me that boarding pupils were orphans, but I didn't think this was true.

It was not a large school. Perhaps fifty girls, from six-year-olds to thirteen-year-olds, boarded there, and the single building held them all and classrooms and chapels and nuns besides. The school occupied a block; behind the building there were a yard with spaces marked off for games and an adjoining garden with a grotto to the Virgin Mary built of big, clumsy stones. The girls in the first three grades could go only in the yard or in the building; but during the day we were joined by day pupils, both boys and girls, for classes and games. These others presumably lived near the school — some of them may have lived no more than a block away — but for me the world outside the school's walls ceased to exist. I was completely incurious about the homes of the day pupils. Yet every doorway and statue and stone ornament and pebble of the school was of the greatest interest, and I was always touching, smelling, even — when no one was looking — tasting a patch of brass or a knob of wood. I remember the tin that covered a big table in the basement — a sheet of tin folded under the edges of the table and tacked into place. On that table were laid slices of bread spread with margarine and apricot jam for the morning collation. I remember the word "collation" — a new word, long and full of sound and having a pleasant meaning. I passed my hand along the smooth blood-red brick until it reached the basement window; then I bent down and watched the kitchen girls laying out slices of bread, the top of each slice like the top of a valentine heart.

I remember the Virgin Mary's bare foot pressing the head of a serpent.

I remember how we walked two by two in front of Sister Stephen to the Cathedral on Sunday to hear Mass. Patsy told me that if I rubbed my hands together and then blew on them, they would get warm; I still do this, even though it does not warm my hands — perhaps I do it because I liked Patsy.

Now and then the older girls — the thirteen-year-olds, I suppose — said they would brush and braid our hair, and this was a particular treat because their dormitory was redolent of privilege: each girl had a dresser twice as large as mine and a screen of white cloth to form a cubicle about her bed. The privacy of those cubicles seemed to me the most desirable thing in the world from the first moment I saw them.

A fat girl with a pageboy lifted me onto a stool: "What've you got to say for yourself?" and began to brush my hair, grabbing a handful in her fist and brushing it until the brush crackled and stray hairs, alive with electricity, crawled over my cheek and down my neck. I hated it; and in order not to think about it I imagined having a cubicle of my own, a curtained and inviolable space. I could read there, or cry. At night, in our dormitory, there was a dim light, and when somebody was crying anybody could see her. If the crying went on, eventually a light would go on behind the screen at the end of the room, a shadow would rise in silhouette behind the screen, and then Sister Stephen appeared in shawl and nightdress and stamped through the dormitory to the weeper's bedside: "Wake up. You're having a nightmare. Hush now. Go back to sleep." A few times somebody admitted that she wanted her mother. "Your mother isn't here,"

Sister Stephen said, her voice like a stick: she was teaching us something about the world. How quickly we learned what she taught us!

"Do you want me to tell you a story?" said the girl who was brushing my hair.

"Yes," I said, pleased. I knew what kind of story she would tell.

"This is a true story, now," the girl said. The brush went down my hair very, very slowly. "There was this fraternity and they wanted to test the new members, you know? So they found this big old, awful old haunted house, really spooky, and they said to the boys, 'You have to spend the night in this old haunted house.' And meanwhile they got a medical student to give them the arm of this black man and they hung up the black man's arm in the house and made voices going, 'I want my arm back!' And the next day they went in and found one of the boys was dead and the other was crazy and his hair had turned white just overnight —"

"Tell me another story."

The older girls also knew a story about people who strapped panthers' claws to their hands and murdered travelers, and a story about a man who fell into a hay-baling machine. The little girls screamed when they listened to these stories; then, with our hair brushed and braided and the braids tied with elastic and plaid ribbons, we walked back to our own dormitory and waited for Sister Stephen to lead us downstairs to breakfast.

That year the snow began early, in the middle of October, and it was decided that I was too sickly — or too likely to be sickly — to be allowed to play in the snow. I had not been sick and I resented this confinement; but now it seems more reasonable to me, for I must have become, in those few weeks at Saint Agnes', an unprepossessing and listless child. I was infected with a sort of nervous apathy: I cried a good deal and played with my food and daydreamed and did not listen the first time. "I want you to hear me the first time!" Sister Stephen insisted. For some reason I still find inexplicable she wanted us to have spirit. She liked disobedience, and I remember the cold look with which she took her leave of me when the day's lessons were over and I stayed behind in the classroom while the other children went to play in the snow. "Goodbye, Sister," I said.

"Goodbye," she said. "Turn out the light." She waited a moment, frowned at me, as if to provoke me to something — to demand I be allowed outside? I went to the window and leaned on the sill. From the second-story classroom window I could see the snow gather under the lights in the schoolyard. Children in snowsuits made snowmen and threw snowballs and lay down in the untrodden patches and waved their arms to make angels. Standing in the window, I waved my arms too, imagining the soft resistance of the snow. A long time later a buzzer sounded loudly: the voice of the building. The little figures in snowsuits left the yard and disappeared through the lighted doorway.

But eventually I disobeyed. I don't remember how. Probably I whispered when we were supposed to be silent or didn't pay attention or wriggled in my seat in class — a lot of time was spent ordering children not to wriggle. Not to sway back and forth behind their desks, or curl their feet up under them or shift from spot to spot on the curved oak seat. In any event, a day came when we were told that our class would get to see a cartoon film, and after lessons we were led down the hall not to the dormitory but toward the stairs: "up there" the film would be shown. And then something hap-

pened and then Sister Stephen suddenly pulled me out of
the line and held me immobile while the others passed.

"I warned you," she said.

"I won't do it again," I said, already having forgotten what
I'd done.

"But you did do it again! You disobeyed me deliberately!"
She jerked my arm, and I flung up my hands and cried,
Please. And then the combination of her own anger and my
cowardice carried her past the edge of reason and she slapped
my face with the back of her hand and cried, "There! And
if your nose bleeds, don't blame me!" My nose began to bleed
at once, and she shoved me into an empty classroom and
went out, locking the door behind her. I was used to my nose
bleeding and it did not frighten me, but the blow had filled
me with a drowning sense of terror, and I wept and coughed,
covering my face and hands with blood. Some time later an
elderly nun came in to me and led me to the bathroom and
told me to wash my face. I looked in the mirror and saw
blood all over my mouth and hands.

"Now wash your face," she said. Her voice was kind and
she touched ·my face very gently with a rag dipped in warm
water. "If you cry your nose will bleed again."

"Sister Stephen hit me," I said. She frowned at my tattling;
then she told me that I was all right, that I should be good,
and that things were all better now. She was puzzled, I think,
and she did not bring me back to Sister Stephen at once but
walked me to the dormitory, which was empty and dark.
"You won't be afraid if I leave you here?" she asked. "No,"
I said, truthfully, and without another word, without thanks,
I left her and went to my bed and lay down and listened to
her footsteps walk away.

When the other little girls came back, I said nothing and
they asked me no questions — nor did I expect any, and it is

only now that I realize how odd it was that there were no friendships among the little girls. We had lost interest in other human beings. Three or four girls began to wet their beds again. One tall, big-eared girl would go into fits of hysterical anger and bite whomever was nearest her. The worst day was laundry day: our stockings and garters, pants and undershirts, petticoats and nightgowns were all thrown into a large cloth laundry bag. We had to stand silently while Sister Stephen inspected these clothes for signs of wear or worse. One day she reached into the bag, pulled out a pair of pants, read the name tag, and then waved the pants for all to see: "This little girl does not know how to wipe herself properly. She is *filthy.*" And then she pointed at a chunky, red-headed little girl with a boyish face: "These are *yours.* I don't want to see this nasty sort of thing again." All the color went out of the red-headed girl's face, making her freckles seem like the marks of a disease. Sister Stephen flung the pants back in the bag, picked it up and left the room, while the rest of us started to chant, "Nasty! Nasty! Nasty!" The red-headed girl walked over to her bed and hung onto the covers with both hands and cried, while the rest of us, silent now, stared at her — at the small shoulder blades, like the back of a young frog.

It took a while, but one by one we learned that Sister Stephen was pleased when somebody received a gift from home. The red-headed girl, for instance, got a tin weaving frame: a square of tin like a fence for a doll's house, the tin cut into teeth so that yarn could be woven back and forth and up and down. When you finished a hundred squares you could make a blanket, she said. Sister Stephen was delighted with this: she helped the red-headed girl to thread the loom and showed her how to weave the piece of looped wire that served as a bobbin through the warp of green wool. The red-headed girl was allowed to work with her little loom for a few minutes every night after we all got undressed and into our nightgowns; but when she had made two or three squares and lost interest, Sister Stephen lost interest in her and again scolded her as readily as she scolded the rest of us.

My turn came when one of my aunts sent me a pair of small plaster angels — baby angels, one in pink and one in blue, kneeling in prayer. "Aren't these wonderful!" Sister Stephen said. "You must show them to everybody." And I passed them around and now the other little girls were indifferent, while Sister Stephen was full of enthusiasm. "They're lovely!" she said, and her big farm-girl's face got quite pink. "Put them on your dresser where we can see them!"

As a consequence, when our parents came on Sundays we begged for gifts. "I want a paint set." "Can I have a little teeny doll?" One or two girls had already been taken away from the school. The other mothers were uneasy.

"Are you having a good time?" my mother asked me again.

"Oh, yes," I said. I had begun to dread this question.

"I brought you a paint set," she said.

"Thank you!" I said. The first thing I did when she left was to show the paint set to Sister Stephen, who smiled and admired the wide choice of colors.

I wish I could explain Sister Stephen. I can see her: a big woman in a heavy serge habit, with big freckled hands, a big face, seemingly without eyebrows or lashes because these were so pale, and huge blue eyes: so large, so blue and enormous the pupils, that I was sickened by them — by their enormous stare. Sometimes when the light from a window touched her face her eyes were so opaquely blue, so huge, that she seemed blind, like a marble statue. She had a heavy voice and stood habitually with her arms folded and her chin tucked down against the hard white edge of the wimple.

But of her nature, I can only guess. She seemed ruder, more excitable, than the other nuns, and I would hazard now that she was a farm girl from somewhere in the Midwest, and ill-at-ease and resentful among the half-hearted Catholics of the West, who even got along with Protestants and Mormons. It is so easy to imagine wearying, uncomfortable visits from the old bishop, Bishop Gleeson, to the shabby drawing room the sisters kept for themselves. Bishop Gleeson was of my grandmother's time, and he would remember when Saint Agnes' School was full of the daughters of silver kings and copper kings. All up and down Bannock their houses stood: silver mines, copper mines, gold mines paid for the portes-cochère and the turrets and piazzas. Gold from Idaho City plated the cross on Saint Agnes' tower. But now the mines were closed. Up in the mountains snow falls on the fenced, abandoned workings; watchmen sit in their houses looking at the snow fall on the road — tonight they'll call the city to say they're closing it up for the winter. The daughters of the silver kings are old women and spend the winter in Palm Springs.

Sister Stephen stares at the Bishop, amazed he cannot tell the difference between his time and hers. She could walk him to the window some Sunday and show him the sort of people who have their kids in Saint Agnes' School: divorced women, farmers from away up country, people who've had a girl go wild on them. Even the Basques, when they get a little money ahead, send their children to the Sacred Heart sisters in Portland.

And so, when a mother or a relative sends a child a gift, Sister Stephen is reassured that the child has not been forgotten, that *she* has not been forgotten, left thankless with a few little girls whose parents have abandoned them. If a child has no visitors, if no cards or gifts come, Sister Stephen is repelled: what has happened to the child? what perversion of life does the child represent? Every night she tells the little girls to kneel and to pray, and her strong voice urges their voices louder. But nothing happens, no extraordinary grace is shed upon the school or the children or her own bewildered spirit.

At Christmas my mother and her new beau took me to my grandparents' house, and there I found all the grown-ups full of nervous optimism because this was the first Christmas after the War: "We can be thankful at least the War's over," they said to each other. The snow fell and fell past the windows and covered the lawns. "Of course you can play in the snow!" they said to me, and wrapped in a rabbit fur coat I was handed to my cousins, who put me on their sleds and pulled me over hillocky gardens and brought me home again. "There you are!" my grandmother exclaimed. The rabbit fur coat lay on the blue Chinese rug, I was led to the kitchen, right up to the woodstove, my height, fat, hot, my grandfather lifted the stove lid and dropped in a handful of pine needles "for the smell" and then on top of the lid went a kettle "for a toddy." My Uncle Dwight came in from the back porch, smoking a cigar, and I could hear his hunting dogs pawing and slipping on the linoleum of the porch. "We'll fix you a toddy," Uncle Dwight said; he put a teaspoon of bourbon in a glass tumbler and picked up the teakettle. "But first," he said, putting the kettle back on the stove. "First let's have something extra special in this." He opened a cupboard, brought out a little cardboard box, and shook two pieces of rock candy into my hand. "What do you say we put this in?"

"Not all of it."

"Then one piece," and he dropped one piece, big sugar crystals clustered on a string, into the tumbler, covered it with boiling water, gave it to me: "Here's your toddy now." And delighted by the sweet smell of bourbon, I dropped the other piece in and fished it out again. "That'll make you sleep now," he said.

I slept, under a down satin comforter, and woke up in the night sometimes to find myself alone; then I would get out of bed and go first to the window where I could see the light from the front parlor falling across the snow, and then to the door, where I could hear the grown-ups' voices chattering on and on — not their words, but the rising and falling tones, the musical shape of questions and silences.

Sometimes when I was eating breakfast my grandmother asked me if I wanted to play with Bobby Lyons or Norma Mary Metz, but I said I didn't want to.

"Just before you came Norma Mary asked if you'd be here for Christmas," my grandmother said.

"She has so many friends at school," my mother said.

"Yes," I said.

"You'll see them again soon," my grandmother said.

"Yes I will."

"She misses them," my mother said.

Finally they convinced themselves that I missed my school friends very much, and so late New Year's Day my mother and her new beau drove me back to Sand River and Saint Agnes' School. When we started to get out of the car, my mother's eyes filled with tears. "I wish you didn't have to go back so soon," she said, and looked at me imploringly.

"I don't have to go back now," I said.

"Yes, but I know you want to," she said, and with a little snuffle she brushed away the two tears and licked her lips and led me briskly up the walk. A nun I'd seen very seldom answered the bell: "Why what an early bird!" she said. "Have you had your supper?" she asked when my mother had left.

"Yes, Sister."

"Well what will we do with you?"

I was, it seemed, the only girl who had come back yet.

"Wait here," she said, and after a long time Sister Stephen came down the stairs.

"The other girls aren't back yet," Sister Stephen said. "I don't know what we're supposed to do with you." She picked up my suitcase. "You'll have to go to bed." Then she led me up to the dormitory and stood silently in the doorway as I unpacked my case and undressed. She led me to the bathroom. She led me back to the dormitory. She listened to my prayers. "Goodnight," she said, and walked off down the hall. I lay awake for a long time, listening for voices, but I heard nothing but the whispers of the radiators.

The next morning, after a solitary breakfast in the kitchen, I was told I could play in the basement recreation room — a large, low-ceilinged room with a bare floor and three sagging couches, crooked lamps, tables, jigsaw puzzles in half-broken boxes, and squinting windows covered with heavy screens.

The day wore and wore. There was soup for lunch.

"Is anybody back?" I asked the cook.

"Nobody yet," she said. "Look at the snow, will you?" As soon as she said it, the snow stopped too. I went back to the recreation room to play with a jigsaw puzzle, but it was too difficult for me. I climbed up on the back of one of the couches so that I could look out a window. The floor creaked and Sister Stephen came into the room. "Get off that sofa," she said. "Who said you could do that?"

"Nobody," I said.

"Do you think you can climb on furniture?"

"No," I said. "I'm sorry."

" 'No, Sister,' " she said.

"Why are they all gone, Sister?" I asked her.

"They're home with their families because the term hasn't started," she said. "Do you think you can climb on sofas at home?"

"Then why am I here?" I asked.

"You're here because your mother doesn't want you," she said. "You're a bad girl and she doesn't want you."

Then she walked away.

I was nailed to the spot with humiliation; the other girls would come back and discover this awful secret. They would make fun of me — they might even make fun of my mother! because she had made such a mistake, letting Sister Stephen know. All the presents in the world: embroidery frames, paintboxes, holy cards, figurines, miraculous medals — all were worthless, nothing could ransom my humiliation. Looking at the seam of snow across the window I felt a chill, a hot, dreamy chill, rush under my skin as if it were transparent. The next day, when the others came back, I caught a cold.

For several days I would not admit it. Everybody seemed sickly. As we bumped into each other on the processions from dormitory to bathroom, from dining room to classroom, I felt hot breath on my face, the hectic warmth of other bodies. My heart caught cold first: it bumped faster and faster, it lurched awkwardly when Sister Stephen moved close to me, when her habit shadowed the corner of my eye and her cold hand pressed my shoulder: "Pay attention," she said. "Watch where you're going." It was very cold now and the old furnaces were not adequate, and sometimes at night one little girl or another, her face hot and her feet cold, would droop exhausted over the white washbasin and squirt hysterical tears while the toothbrush went around and around in her mouth. "You're acting like a big baby!" Sister Stephen cried in outrage. We all understood this and agreed with her. I, for one, lay in bed silently haranguing my guardian angel: he could and must help me not to be a baby. After a while I could feel his wings close around me — thick, soft and heavy like the wings of wild geese my Uncle Dwight shot — and I swooned into their powdery darkness.

My breath got squeaky, my voice faded.

"What's the matter with you?" Sister Stephen demanded.

"Nothing, Sister," I said, and shut my mouth tight.

And then one day after dinner she took one girl by the back of her collar and stretched her to her toes, inviting us to look at her unfastened garter, unravelled braid, dirty hands and spotted knees. "You are here," said Sister Stephen, "because your mother doesn't want to take care of you, and you can't take care of yourself."

I peeked sideways and other girls were peeking too, partly relieved because our shame was now shared, partly the more hopeless because obviously this was why we were all here, our sentences were not arbitrary or mistaken . . .

"Your mother doesn't want you," said Sister Stephen, early and often; she was no longer informing us of this fact but reminding us. I began to have a dream about my Aunt Bernice: we were driving in her car and the door on my side fell open and I started to fall out. I begged and begged Aunt Bernice to stop the car, to slow down at least so that I could close the door, but she refused and began to wrestle with me and at last I realized that she wanted me to fall out of the car; then I began to scream at her, that she must not do that because my mother would be angry with her — but by that time

Aunt Bernice had turned into an enormous dead dog and lay inert and cold in the meadow grass. In another dream I walked up to a mirror and looked at my face and it had become a hollow shell, like a Halloween mask, the skin all tight, yellow and stiff like an empty bug's carcass left in a spider web. I sat up in bed shrieking. But I made no sound. The dormitory was silent. I waited and waited for the light to go on behind the screen but it did not go on.

"What's the matter with you?" Sister Stephen asked anyway.

I tried to say "nothing," but this time I coughed instead. She put her big cold hand on my forehead and then told me to go to bed. That afternoon the bare trees wobbled behind the windows whenever I woke up. After I had been awake for a few minutes, I began to cough again. Finally Sister Stephen brought me a glass of water. "Don't cough," she said.

I didn't blame her for hating my coughs. They began as a little trickling in my throat, like the small pebbles and dust particles that precede an avalanche; then suddenly my whole chest seemed to cave in with explosions of noise. The coughs were like shouts, and after each paroxysm I was scared and worn out. I sipped at the tepid, musty water. My eyes felt as if I had been staring at the sun.

That night I woke up and began to cough. The noise was unbearably loud. I crammed sheets into my mouth and sucked at the wet, spitty linen. At the end of the dormitory the light went on. She came to me wearing a long, coarse white nightgown, with her hair hanging down the back of her neck and a flashlight in her hand. After telling me to drink some water she shone the light in my face; when I coughed again she whispered furiously, "You're just doing this to annoy me."

"I can't help it," I whined.

"Stop it!"

I tried. A cough expanded in my chest now like a broken steel spring. I pressed my lips together but it was too strong, it broke loose, and I began to cry.

"You can't sleep here, disturbing everybody," she said. "Put on your robe and your slippers."

I did as I was told and followed her out of the dormitory and into a smaller room where there was only one bed.

"This is the infirmary," she said.

It was a fine place. My meals came on trays, and nuns and a doctor and two jigsaw puzzles came to my room. When the door was shut for the night I could lie back on the pillows and cough as long and as loudly as I had to. Then my mother came and said I could come home for a few days.

"I like it here," I said, one jigsaw puzzle to go.

"I know, but it will only be for a few days," she said.

The next morning one of the older girls helped me put on my clothes and braided my hair and led me up the stairs that wound toward the bell tower, past windows that were like lightning flashes, showing bare trees and chimneys crowned with snow. We found my blue tin trunk amidst the others, but we took only my suitcase; yet I pretended I was leaving forever and longed to make the older girl believe this. As we went downstairs the stairway seemed to grow larger with my imagined sense of freedom. In the dormitory I emptied the drawers of my dresser and wrapped the plaster angels in a clean petticoat. "Goodbye," I said to everybody. My mother and Aunt Bernice were in the hall, waiting to take me away. When we went out the door the air carried an electric smell from the fallen snow.

It was the middle of a winter afternoon. I was sitting on the rug in the middle of the living room in Aunt Bernice's house, looking at *The Book of Knowledge*. The pages were heavy and shiny; they reflected the long-slanting sunlight. My mother came into the room and knelt down on the rug.

"Do you miss your friends at school?" she asked.

"No," I said.

"Don't you want to see Sister Stephen?" she asked.

"No," I said.

I began to turn the pages of the book with deliberate slowness so that everything would seem all right and normal, because then I could say — and said — "Sister Stephen slapped me. She made my nose bleed and said it wasn't her fault but it was her fault. She said you didn't want me. She says that to everybody when you do something wrong, she says your mother doesn't want you, right in front of everybody."

My mother jumped up and said in a cold voice, "You aren't going back to that school. That's settled. That's all finished."

Then I wanted to tell her the story again, but she told me that it was finished, that she promised I would never have to go back there again, and so I kept quiet. When several days passed I asked again if I had to go back to the school and she said no again. Finally one evening she came back from downtown and said she had been to the school to tell the Sister Superior about Sister Stephen and that it turned out Sister Stephen was tired and didn't like to take care of children. "Poor thing," my mother said to Aunt Bernice. "The poor woman is —" and then tapped her finger on her temple. "They won't let her take care of any children any more, believe you me."

"But they didn't do anything," I said — or burst out with,

rather, thinking I *knew,* I *knew* what had happened, only *I* knew.

"They didn't know," Aunt Bernice said.

Two years later Saint Agnes' School stopped taking boarding students.

I went to another school and had a good time, but I could not forget Sister Stephen. One night I took out the plaster angels and smashed them with a hammer, but this made me feel worse than ever. Then I began to have the dream I would have for years: I found myself back in the school, but up in the bell tower, high above the moonlit snow and the black tree boughs, and I ran down the dark stairways and through the yellow-electric halls, putting the nuns to flight and waking up all the little girls in their white nightgowns and chasing them into a fire slide like the one on the Warshaw School.

And then I must tell one more dream. A few years ago I was explaining the idea of purgatory to somebody, and I remembered how Sister Stephen explained it: each sin, she said, was like a nail driven into a clean white plank. One could remove the nail but the scar was still there. That night I dreamt there was something in my breast: an arrow, a burning point of light. Then my mother died and the arrow fell out of my breast and grew dimmer, dimmer and winked out. Sister Stephen was there and I begged and begged but she would not speak to me.

"They tore down Saint Agnes' School," I said, when I went back to Sand River. "There's nothing left."

"No," my cousin Joan said indifferently.

Soldier, Soldier

> There is another personage, — a personage less im-
> posing in the eyes of some, perhaps insignificant.
> The schoolmaster is abroad, and I trust to him,
> armed with his primer, against the soldier in full
> military array.
>
> — *Lord Brougham*

Everybody was embarrassed when Nicholas returned alive
from Vietnam. That he had gone at all placed upon him a
double stigma: coward and fool. He had regarded with dis-
interest — not contempt, although it was, in the eye of the
beholder, hardly distinguishable — the athletic exertions of
his friends who evaded the draft. They bribed psychiatrists.
They were certified for unexpected structural flaws: skewed
collarbones and defective hearts. There was a party one night
where a little boy who was expecting his physical in the
morning got drunk and tried to show his friends how he'd
play a homosexual. It was embarrassingly bad — what was he
more afraid of? being a homosexual or being killed? Then
he got a lot drunker and rubbed his swollen crotch against
the host's sister: everybody said, later, that he was in his way
a casualty of war.

Nicholas himself had been present at one or two of the
clandestine bon voyage (pour toujours) parties thrown at
the airport for "new Canadians." Everybody was so casual in
pantomime ("See you in a week! Have a nice vacation!") and
the new Canadian and his wife or girlfriend stood, sickened,

in their brand new square clothes — his hair cut off, his face pale, his hand pressing, pressing the cheap new necktie. What would they do in Canada? for news came back that Canada was petty and stuffy. A girl began to cry. Then her histrionics overcame her: real hysterics. She had to be led to the women's toilets, where she threw up. "Jesus Christ," said Nicholas. "It's a wonder we're not all busted." The new Canadians finally left, to everybody's relief. For . . .

. . . it had to be faced: there was in fact no way to "beat the draft." Most of Nicholas' friends were, in theory at least, draft exempt: students or teachers. Every once in a while Nemesis — there was no other word for it — snatched someone. It was unsafe (everybody agreed) to have been in ROTC. A couple of good family men, a Chaucerian and a History of Science, were, well almost, drafted. Or so close to being drafted, rescued only at the last minute by frightened exchanges of letters, pricey consultations with lawyers — why, they might as well have gone: "I aged ten years." And then a couple of people really were drafted. Nobody remembered their names. And some undergraduates, victims of their own inability to perform brilliantly enough. They came to office hours like cattle milling around a stockyard, their eyes dulled, unable at last even to beg. Nobody begged who was really draft-eligible. The ones who begged always had trick knees up their pantlegs, so to speak, and used their demands as one more club across their instructors' reluctant shoulders, as if to say, Why *can't* you make me smart or diligent or, for that matter, even likable?

So — when Nicholas was, well, not drafted, drawn into the army, like a piece of fluff up a vacuum cleaner, it was considered his own fault. What was he doing, anyway, a loose piece of fluff, to be picked up? Foolishly, he'd finished his thesis. Foolishly, he'd been in ROTC. He had given wonderful parties, catered them so well that a number of people thought he was queer; and thus they reasoned that if he didn't mind being considered queer by many of his friends, why should he mind being considered queer by the army? "Very strange guy," said several persons. Those who knew him a little better knew, or learned, or were told by him (they could never remember exactly how they knew this) that his being in the army was simply a fuck-up. Nicholas was a wheeler-dealer. Every summer for five years he went to Europe, and every summer he came back with a new car or rare books or unusual prints, which he then traded away, making more deals. It was said he'd never paid rent. It was said he'd never paid as much rent as other people. His family was very rich, and so he had the resources to live thriftily, turning little deals to his own advantage. At any rate, he'd tried this with the army, dreaming perhaps of a billet in Heidelberg. The army proved too ponderous for his skills: like an elephant rolling on an inexperienced ringmaster — unarguable.

He was sent to Vietnam. He sent postcards from Kyoto where he'd gone on his first leave. Kyoto, he wrote, was marvelous. Then there were no more postcards. By degrees his name and memory were smudged by the bad news from Vietnam.

Every time somebody took a plane he found himself sitting next to a soldier or a marine who trustingly, earnestly described the filthiness of the war: black market stuff, clumsy killings, predatory whores, the bored and spiteful Vietnamese bourgeoisie sending money to Switzerland.

"Nicholas is in Vietnam," said several persons, accusingly: it was too much to expect that he would remain uncorrupted. And then, by sheer bad luck, he got his name in the papers: away from the front, lounging in a back street hotel in Saigon, he'd found himself in the midst of a street-to-street battle with a small infiltration force of Viet Cong. The hotel was full of screaming mothers, panicky Chinese shopkeepers, bewildered soldiers on passes, and Nicholas, *faute de mieux,* had picked up a rifle to defend himself and therefore the hotel. With some success. Not quite a hero: he had been too unquestionably on the defensive, he had called down no artillery fire on his own men (or women, as the case happened to be), had not run forward with grenades in both hands, had thrown himself on no machine guns. He simply huddled on the balcony of the *Olympia* and duelled with the enemy. It made a nice picture. "For God's sake, that's *Nicholas!*" his friends exclaimed when they looked at their papers. For some it was the final condemnation of the war. If Nicholas was there, and fighting, then the war was irredeemably absurd. It was as if they had been told that the Defense Department was arming chicken hawks, or dropping buttered bread to stop truck convoys. If Nicholas was firing a gun, why, anybody might be doing it. But everybody else clearly wasn't. Nicholas was forgotten, angrily.

"Guess who I saw on the street today? *Nicholas!*"
"Are you sure?"
"Oh, yes . . ."
"I don't know what to say."
He was seen. His presence was reported. He was *back*: the only one known to be so. Lately a number of people had come *from* Vietnam. They had no pasts. One assumed, if anything, that their whole lives had been aimed at their presence in Vietnam; spent, like bullets, denuded (where was the cartridge case? or were they the cartridge cases?) they rebounded into college, objects of curiosity among the undergraduates. Inscrutable because so rudely transparent,

like shop windows: behind their mild eyes winked the reply, "It's a dumb war." They had seen, they had been trained (one presumed) to fight it. But Nicholas, as everyone knew, had not been trained to fight. Unless, as several persons suspected, he had in fact been *all along* an agent of the government! His academic slatternliness was a *ruse!* One had it on good authority that he wasn't queer — he just came from Beverly Hills, and his melodious voice was legitimately acquired. He might be a rough-neck at heart.

He was back, and therefore regarded as a stranger. It was inevitable, several persons said, that he should have changed. No demonstration of that fact was necessary.

Nola hated the war, easily. To her it was as palpable as, say, an unfair matron at a boarding school. You might be walking down the street on a sunny day listening for the birds, feeling generous, and yet you were always aware that the war was going to spoil something soon. It was like an infected conscience: hot, puffy, going bad. The restaurants kept pasting tiny squares of paper over the old prices. Poor people stood up on television and asked for Easter coats for their children, more food and clean houses. "Oh, no," the rich people said. "We can't afford that." The newspapers tried to report the events of the war, but they made no sense. Every now and then Nola would ask some sensible, serious, studious acquaintance, "We're losing the war, aren't we?" "Yes," he would reply. "I *thought* so . . ." Nola would complain. Yet men of experience and education said publicly that the war was going well. The generals said so. The presidents said so. The enemy soldiers, guerrillas and civilians were dying by the thousands; there were *always* more casualties on their side than on ours. Always. For this, and similar reasons, the newspapers made no sense.

Nola had taken a year off to study city planning. She couldn't quite afford it (something else she blamed on the war) and she couldn't quite plan cities, either, as she discovered. She was drifting sideways toward a job with the city; lots of clever friends worked for the city: it was a well-paying good deed, to dedicate yourself to the task of keeping the city a fun place to live in. Much more fun if you weren't robbed or raped or hit by a sniper — and these things happened naturally because nobody could afford to stop them. The money was all going into the war. What good was it to get a high salary if you might be robbed or raped at any moment? But Nola hadn't settled into a job; she was drifting toward it, like an ornamental balloon; there was no hurrying her. She was busy enough, after all: the man she was living with was one of the organizers of the local Resistance.

So it wasn't mere fashion, that she hated the war.

Some nights they came home to his apartment and learned, from the neighbors, that the landlord had been searching the place. They laid traps for the landlord, but he sprang them arrogantly. He was, he told his other tenants, a patriot. Mike got furious the first time and then subsided; it did not really matter to him that the landlord prowled through his apartment, looking for crumbs to give to the FBI. Mike had given up privacy. The telephone was too obviously tapped; it rattled and echoed, and it was embarrassing how easily they could correct a bad connection just by shouting "get off the line, FBI creeps!" Friends complained of the swollen or puckered condition of Mike's letters. His mother sent him candied fruit from San Diego and the boxes, the pride of Mission Pak, were slit open, eviscerated, rudely repacked. Mike had not a touch of paranoia, and Nola was first angered and then bemused by the fact that his life — and thus, hers — could be so violated, pried into, and yet fundamentally unchanged. Mike made only the slightest adjustments to acknowledge the presence of his observers. She tried to follow his example, but uncomfortably, as if he were a practiced nudist leading her, still uncertain, into Sunland Park. She felt modest. Secrets stuck in her throat. Mike had secrets too, but he was smug about them. They were in a locker somewhere, as it were, and he had mailed the key to himself.

"What will you do if they call you up?" she asked, many times.

"Leave the country," he said, without hesitation.

At Christmas they left the country together: they went to Mexico. He needed rest and sunlight. "Mexico eats it," he said, on the third day, *a propos* their hotel room, their meals, and the car rental agency. It was no joke: he disliked Mexico, he disliked the foreign language he could not speak, and he despised the second-rateness he discovered, here and there. "It's no worse than lots of places in the U.S.," she said one day, but Mike retorted that he didn't intend to live in "lots of places" in the U.S. either.

"What will you do if they call you up?" she asked, looking at him looking at a wan enchilàda.

"Leave the country," he said, infuriated.

Furiously he mounted her in bed. Mumbling, grumbling, muttering. She had a clear *idea* of what role she should play there. The idea, of course, had a slight deadening effect, but so, she'd heard, had condoms — yet people used them, once, for the sake of the relationship. "I am an ocean," she thought to herself. Her idea directed her to rock, to billow, to ebb, to spring. She tried to imitate the Mexican girls' walk (it was the one aspect of the country that seemed to please Mike). She rubbed his back. She loved him, sincerely, and if she got a measured amount of pleasure from him firsthand, this was matched by the pleasure she gave him reflected (finally) from his satisfied face, his trusting sleep. She was also jealous of the war because it engaged his feelings, like an old girlfriend, not quite worthy of him, who'd rejected him.

When they came back from Mexico he began to make public speeches, and he discovered he could do this well. But it was too late, his pride had been abandoned, and it could not be enhanced. "That speech was marvelous!" Nola said, and he got a flash of pleasure from her praise. But a flash only. Then she realized what had happened; he had despaired. Naturally quick, energetic and clever, he worked and worked for the war resistance movement, but only because he was naturally restless. He did not believe they could do any good. The telephone taps, the opened mail, the landlord's snooping were *only jokes*. Nola envied him. When she recognized his despair — and it had authority, it informed her: "No use" — she did not feel energetic anymore. She wanted to get away or do something else or do something desperate.

"It's got to be done," he said. Every other evening now he bought a new bottle of gin, and they ended the days by drinking and listening to Otis Redding and sleepily making love. Well, sort of love.

"What are you thinking?" she said to his mutterings.

"I don't know." He laughed, he fell asleep.

"Damn it!" she said. "I don't know what you want anymore!"

She decided that he had no further right to her compliance: if he were not really angry but despaired instead, if the mutterings were no longer outrage comforting itself in her but *habit* . . . She was a puritan, although she didn't know it: sexual *habits* seemed to her obscene. "Animal" she might have said, off her guard.

Inevitably they fell out of love. He found a girl who, apparently, liked his habits. Nola collected her goldfish, her books, her kitchen utensils and her clothes — including even the peignoir (very expensive) which she'd inherited, as it were, from the girl who'd preceded her in Mike's affections. As far as she could tell, Mike had never noticed its reappearance on her; she wondered if she had left it, and if the new girl took to wearing it, whether he would have noticed at last that it was being passed from girl to girl. She would not know; she was finished with Mike. It was one more thing to blame on the war.

One morning when it was hot and rainy Nola looked across the street and saw a familiar face and waved. When he waved back she realized who it was ("Nicholas!") and she blushed. Nicholas crossed the street, heedless of parked cars and moving cars alike, and said, "Nola, I'm glad to see you again." She shook hands with him (bravely, she thought) and said they must have coffee sometime. "Right now," he said, smiling intently. His smile took her interest: she could not remember his smiling in quite that way before he went to Vietnam. It was a small, steady smile, with faintly worried eyes, the smile of somebody listening to a foreign language and smiling to reassure: "Yes, I'm listening, I'm trying to understand, don't worry. I almost understand." He seemed to be trying to understand her and she hadn't spoken to him more than a dozen words. Maybe the army had taught him to smile like that. "Yes, let's have some coffee," she said.

It turned out he wanted somebody to talk to: his cousin in Portland wanted him to become a financial partner in a medical laboratory. Nicholas had first thought he should do it and go to medical school and become a doctor, but now, a couple of hours later, he wondered if this was a good time to invest in anything at all.

"I hope you're not in the market," he said earnestly. "I mean, you won't be offended when I say this, but I don't imagine you have a lot of money to spare, and if you can't spare the *time* to sit in your broker's office, you're likely to lose everything you invest."

"I'm not in the market," she said.

The next day was hot and rainy too, and the next day. Nola stayed home and wore nothing but a bathrobe. She washed her hair and shaved her legs and painted her toenails the color of plastic baby rattles, but nobody called. Her feet, with their freshly painted toenails, rested on the part of the *New York Review of Books* she hadn't read yet. Studying a full page advertisement for a book on sexual compatibility, she wondered why they ran such ads.

Nicholas found an apartment with a bedroom and a living room. He ordered a telephone and he bought himself a Danish bed. He bought scotch, gin and beer, and invited his friends to come over, to have a pizza with him: the floors had wall-to-wall carpets. "I hate wall-to-wall carpets," he said. "They remind me of Los Angeles," he said, defining the difference between Los Angeles and Beverly Hills. "But I've got a great view, a fantastic view," he said. It was hot and rainy and his friends bore no grudges: "Glad to see you back, man," they said. They told him about their sad lives: their girlfriends were going to therapy groups, their wives were getting bitchy now that the babies were born, and their students weren't wearing bras. "Jesus Christ," Nicholas said, sympathetically. When his friends left his apartment they said to each other they thought he'd changed a lot. Several persons said they didn't want to know what he'd done in

Vietnam. Several persons who did not visit him said they would not do so.

Life magazine printed the photographs of all the American soldiers who had been killed in one week in Vietnam. One hot and rainy morning Nola went to the dentist for an X-ray and she opened this copy of *Life* magazine. The pages were loose and crumpled because so many persons had looked at the pictures. She looked and looked and she couldn't understand why they were there, or, for that matter, why she was in the dentist's office instead of on the page of *Life* magazine. "If I were a man," she said to herself. "If I were a man and if I were dead I would be in *Life*." There was room on those pages for all the men she had ever slept with, danced with, had coffee with, sat beside in college. She studied the faces very carefully but she did not recognize one. Something monstrous occurred to her: for every man's photograph there was a girl, somewhere, who said, "Oh, *no!*" Were there any girls who had said, "Go to Vietnam and fight for your country?" she wondered. She chose one photograph at random and looked at the boy's face and tried to say it: "Go to Vietnam and fight for your country." This made her shake. She put the magazine down. After a while the nurse said it was her turn.

On that afternoon Nola went into Maccoby & Wales and bought a pink cotton knit dress that was cut just like a cotton polo shirt. The saleslady said the dress was "fantastic."

On that afternoon Nicholas ran into Doug Mangels in Discount Records. "What are you up to now, Doug?" asked Nicholas.

"Dodgin' the draft, man," said Doug. "They *say* we may get busted for conspiracy."

"No shit."

"No lie," said Doug. "But listen, I hear, what do I hear, I hear you were *there*. Like, what was it like?"

"Miserable," said Nicholas.

"Yeah," said Doug. "You shouldn't have gone."

"Well now I know. I'm not going again."

"Oh, *yeah* . . ." said Doug. "Well come join the Resistance."

"I'm thinking about that," said Nicholas.

"Like it would really help," said Doug. "You're a veteran, right? You can talk about that. The veterans can really tell it, see."

"I don't like to," Nicholas said. "Like, hell, who would?"

"Sure," Doug said, and then he shut up. He shook Nicholas' hand and walked away, bouncing to the music: ta-ta-ta-ta. Later that afternoon Doug saw Mike and he said, "I saw Nicholas in Discount Records."

"That son of a bitch," Mike said. "He wasn't drafted. He enlisted. Or something like that."

"Yeah? He said he'd join the Resistance."

"What the hell good is it now? He's already *been* there. You see what I mean?"

"I *see*," said Doug.

The conversation went on for over two hours, and all the while it was raining.

When Nicholas left Discount Records he saw Nola carrying a big package from Maccoby & Wales. "Do you need a ride?" Nicholas asked. Yes, she did. They got in his car and she had to wipe the rain off her face. A drop ran down toward her mouth and she caught it with her tongue. "Let me show you my apartment," Nicholas said. Yes, she said.

The rain made it dark but he didn't turn on any lights; the

living room was empty except for a half dozen strongly colored framed prints lying on the rug. He made two weak
drinks. "Which should I hang in here?" he asked Nola, as
they leaned over the pool of shapes. Her face and his face
were reflected in a vermilion paper. "This time I'm going to
spend some money," he said. He looked very apprehensive
when he said this.

"What about the medical laboratory?"

"What's that!" He looked quite alarmed. "Did I tell you
about that? I shouldn't have told you. You haven't told anybody."

"What? Who would I tell?"

"I don't *know*," he said. "Well, I haven't made up my
mind about it. I haven't had time to think. I've had a very
bad week. First that on my mind. Now my sister wants me to
go in with her on a cabin in Vail. But maybe I'll teach: I'll
have to think about that. Then there's this friend of mine
who's been having a fantastically bad time with drugs and
who I keep telling to go see a doctor and she won't do it.
She says she can't trust a doctor. Well who does she think
she can trust? She wants to come over here and talk about it
and I just have one thing to say to her and I've said it."

He stopped talking, as if he'd lost interest in what he was
saying — or as if he were listening for something. He stood
in the kitchen doorway, tall and heavy, looking around the
room. From the street a siren said: wowawowawowawowa.

"I read about you in the paper," she said.

Now he looked at her and smiled. She was so startled that
she looked away.

"What's your job, Nicholas?"

"I'm working for the city."

"Oh, isn't that nice?" Nola said. "Listen, I should be going
back."

"I'll take you back," Nicholas said. "Wait for the rain to stop."

"It's been raining for days." She was annoyed by the weak drink; she'd finished it too quickly, and Nicholas was still working on his. "If I go now you won't have to take me. It's still light."

"I'll take you. Don't rush," Nicholas said. "Listen to my new record. Come in here and listen to my new record." He led her into the bedroom. He sat on the bed and took off his shoes. "Take off your shoes," he said. "Listen to this record." She took off her shoes. They sat side by side on the bed, like toy people, she thought.

"Do you know Dinu Lipatti?" he asked.

"No."

"Listen, listen."

She looked at his hands: how do you hold a rifle? What is it like to hold a rifle?

There was a crack in the record: la-la-*da*-la-la! la-la-*da*-la-la!

"Fuck it," he said.

"I don't want too much furniture in this room," he said, as he fixed the record. "I saw a chest in New York. Long, no legs. Then let me show you what I have." He brought a large box out of the closet; opening the box very carefully he lifted up an Indian dryad carved in cinnamon colored wood. "Of course you see pieces *like* her all the time," he said. "But if you study her you'll see why she's exceptional." The dryad was smiling boldly, her round breasts shone. He reached in the box again and brought out a silver pedestal. "This makes a difference. And let me show you something else." He ran back to the closet and brought out another box and opened it. Yards of Thailand silk, like frozen light, unfolded and unfolded over his arms. Then folded again. The dryad and her silver pedestal went back in the box too.

"I shouldn't have told you about Portland, the laboratory," he said. "Do you want another drink? It would make sense if I had a medical degree. I could be more than a financial partner. But then I should trust my cousin. He's made money before. I should go to Portland, of course. I shouldn't try to settle it on the telephone." Absent-mindedly he put his arms around Nola and hugged her. "I like the rain," he said. "This apartment isn't as gloomy as I thought on a bad day. Just tell me when you want to go home. Or do you want another drink?"

"Another drink," she said, so that he would stop hugging her. She couldn't understand what he was talking about, and she felt ready to jump out of her skin. The rain was pouring and the record was sadhearted and the bare room got on her nerves. But she wanted to know *something* — what was it? She wondered what he wanted to do. Did he want to hug her some more? Had somebody said he was definitely queer, or had they just *thought* he was queer.

He came back with two more weak drinks. "Cheerio," he said. After a couple of swallows he hugged her again. He had big arms, really, and she had never noticed that he was, in fact, a big man, heavy. He had a rubbery face that should have been expressive but wasn't.

"Maybe I ought to paint this room," he said. "What do you think?"

"Were you angry?" she asked.

"No," he said. "What about?" He was *listening* to her, but she didn't have anything to say. She was trying to imagine what it was like, to fire a gun at another human being, to have somebody shooting back at you. It was not her business, it was his business, he had been *taking care of business,* wasn't that somebody's phrase? Whose?

"What did you say?" he asked.

"Nothing," she said. She picked up his hand and kissed it. He took off her clothes. She took off his.

"What are you doing?" she asked.

"Turning off the phone." And a little while later he said, "Ah, fantastic."

Around midnight he turned the phone on again and went out to the kitchen. The phone rang immediately. "Answer it," he said. "Would you please."

"Hello, is Nicholas there?" asked a woman.

It rang again an hour later. "You answer it," Nicholas said.

"Is Nicholas there?" asked a woman. Maybe the same woman, maybe another.

It rang again a few minutes later. He answered it. "Was that the first woman again?" Nola asked.

"What? No, that was an old friend," he said. "Let's go to sleep." After a while he said, "If I could get a month off I'd go to Poland." A little later he said, "What's that funny noise you make? It sounds like a little. I don't know what? Are you all right?"

"I must have been sleeping," she said. She found something, a tear or sweat, on her temple. Why should she have been crying? What was her dream? She was awake, lying in bed with a soldier. Then she went to sleep again, thinking of the war going on and on and on, like a heart beating.

Small Sounds and Tilting Shadows

When I was twenty-one I was half-crazy — I spent myself on that, as if madness were entailed on my maturity. Perhaps it was: I am the youngest child of an elderly family, and when I came along they had already been confined in middle age, convalescing from the strenuous regime of pills, drink, and lawsuits that had cured them of youth.

When I was half-crazy I went to Paris, intending to be old. "Why do you have all these dark dresses?" my boyfriend said. "Look at them: dark green, dark blue, brown. Gray. Black." They lay folded on the bed, with black stockings, black leather shoes, black leather gloves, and handbags fitted with brass and secret locks. I had a diary bound in oilcloth and a letter folder that made a desk of one's lap and dispensed paper, envelopes, and stamps. I had a Swiss knife.

"I'll be with you in a month," my boyfriend said.

I thought he was lying, but now I think perhaps he meant to come, although I didn't want him to. I had a return passage on a ship and no companion; my family didn't even consider the hazards of my traveling alone — they had met no temptations in twenty years. They worried more about sickness and insisted I have all my teeth fixed before I left.

A week after I arrived in Paris I was sick and lay abed while the woman who managed my small hotel brought me broth and tea. I said *Merci,* echoing her voice that was lower and rustier than mine. The bellboy was a little Yugoslav who thought love would cure me. He came late at night and kissed me and brought magazines the guests had left in their rooms; he turned off the lamp and tried to get under the covers. "Ai ahm note ofraid," he said. At last the manageress called a doctor. He listened to my lungs and felt my pulse. *"Mademoiselle,"* he said, *"vous avez la grippe,"* and he ordered a vial of charcoal flavored with licorice.

When I could get out of the hotel again, I came to hate Paris. Although I wore a wrinkled coat, my hair was limp, and my face was spotty, I was followed in the streets and cafés by rat-faced men who usually claimed they had jobs with foreign consulates. When I yelled at them, *Allez!,* I humiliated myself more than them. I fixed on the idea of going to London, where people spoke English, for sometimes my head swam from listening too hard to French and finding words for my replies. *"J'irai, Madame, je voyage en Londres,"* I said to the manageress. *"L'addition, s'il vous plaît."*

In London I looked up all the names in my address book and went to "events." From a bed-and-breakfast hotel near Regent's Park I wrote letters home in my new italic handwriting to say that I was having a wonderful time. Air letters swiftly responded: why wasn't I in Italy? My aunts liked to talk about going to Italy: they took extension courses in the language and subscribed to travel magazines; but Wenona's husband hates airplanes and Vivian's husband, a diabetic, is convinced that there is no adequate medical care in Europe. "I hope you go to Rome," Wenona said in every letter.

But I was contentedly growing older: I bought walking shoes, mackintoshes, and tweed skirts, and with guidebooks and mystery magazines I went to Brighton and Horsham, Canterbury and Ely. The autumn came in languidly, filling the countryside with mists.

One evening in London I was walking out of Regent's

Park when I realized that my stomach hurt and my face was hot. Mr. Wing at the hotel sent me to Doctor Evans, who asked me a good many questions — I had only one: was this *la grippe* again? — and touched me gently here and there and then prodded me until I squeaked. It was appendicitis — he suggested it had always been appendicitis — and the next morning my appendix was gone. Two or three of my new friends came to the hospital and seemed full of concern.

"I can't travel," I said. "They want to send me to a convalescent home."

Then by lucky chance somebody knew somebody else who knew of a flat.

"I can't afford a flat," I said.

"It's rent-free. You'd be caretaker. But you must be prepared to leave on a moment's notice."

"Well, that's no good," I said.

"It'll be weeks before you have to go."

"Then I'll take it," I said.

There are hundreds of squares in London that are indistinguishable from Canon Square, a meanly fenced little park surrounded by Georgian houses, each with its below-stairs rooms made into a "garden flat," with a flight of steps up from the street and staring big windows that the tenants must cover with heavy curtains to keep out the cold. Some of the houses on Canon Square were bed-and-breakfast places. One was a tenement full of Pakistani immigrants. Another (they said at the pub) was a brothel. "Which one?" I asked. Nobody was certain. On the side streets that did not command a view of the park there were cheap cafés and butcher shops, greengrocers, ironmongers. When I first moved to Canon Square, I hobbled, still bent double from my stitches, from shop to shop and satisfied the British taste for grotesquerie.

"This is the lass what lost her appendix!" the greengrocer said to his other customers when I came into his shop. "When are you going to show us the stitches, love?"

"Here, look at this!" the butcher's wife said. She kicked off her shoe to show us a webbed toe. Everybody laughed but me.

Despite the discomforts of walking bent over, I stayed out much of the day. Partly it was the sheer inconvenience of the place, for the flat was at the very top of the house and there was no elevator, only steep, uncarpeted stairs. The rooms were low and had whitewashed walls and dark gray fitted carpeting. A tiny window in the kitchen looked down on Canon Square and the treetops that were losing their leaves by handfuls. Larger windows in the back rooms looked down into a wasted garden, across to other rooftops and chimneys. I bought flowers, several bunches at a time, but their color was lost in the dim white light of the rooms.

"Come back with me," I begged friends and acquaintances. "Let me fix you a meal. Let me fix you dinner." I turned on all the electric fires and kept the record player going all the time.

"It's a grim sort of place, isn't it," everybody said, sooner or later.

For a week I had an English boyfriend. "Don't mind my stitches," I said. "It doesn't hurt. Stay. Please stay." But as we lay side by side under cold sheets and rough blankets, the eye of the electric fire upon us, we were too much alone; the loneliness sifted between us, like falling snow. Silences blew into drifts and froze solid. At the end of the week he had to go up to Manchester, to see his family. His dad was ill.

The next week I went to a party where I met a big aggressive man who produced programs for the BBC. He sweated as he drank, and he wore a lot of rings. "What will you do with yourself, darling?" he asked, when he'd got my story out of me. "Will you go back to university? Or will you be an air host*ess*? Who are you, tell me that, will you, who are you?" I burst into angry tears. "Why do you want to know?" I said. "You don't care who I am."

"Come on," he said, aiming for a taxi, his flat, his bed. "Come on, darling, it's late."

"No," I said, though I wanted to go with him. It would be cozy in his flat: I imagined lots of magazines and whiskey. But I'll never know: he didn't find it worthwhile to argue with me.

I got into a taxi alone and said, "Canon Square, please," but then I pictured what the flat would look like when I got there. The light from any lamp I switched on would fall in a crisply drawn figure on the carpet; the bedroom had curtains of dark gray velvet, from the floor to the ceiling, and if I did not open them, I could not tell whether it was day or night. Sometimes I went into that room at noon and found myself staring at the shadow of the bed, the unchanging shadows in the curtains. I rapped on the taxi's partition. "Gloucester Terrace," I said. "I'm sorry. I've changed my mind."

A nice boy named Michael lived in Gloucester Terrace — a socialist who ran an office somewhere helping somebody. When I rang the bell, he came to the front door in robe and pajamas. "I'm sorry," I said, "but I couldn't stand to go home. Can I stay here tonight?" He looked at me as if he wanted to say no with all his heart, but he let me in anyway and gave me pajamas and tucked me into a far corner of his bed.

The moon came through the window and shone on the corner of the high-headed bed. It was silent and cold; Michael slept inaudibly, but I lay awake for a long time because I felt safe.

The next day, when I got back to Canon Square, I was obsessed by the big man who wore so many rings. He had asked who I was. I knew who I was, all right — so I said to myself: I am . . . and listening, I heard only water in the pipes, wind rapping on a window, my own sigh.

"Who lives here?" I said out loud.

The flat's leaseholder, the man with his name on the bell, was a Canadian journalist, I'd been told. The flat had come to me from a friend of his, who had been charged with its safekeeping and who had decided to go to Italy instead. I was to keep it clean, dusted, have the window washer in, and keep the cupboards stocked with tinned food. When I was given the key, I had asked: "Where is he? When will he be back?"

"I think — but you mustn't tell anybody — I think he's in China," said the departing buddy.

"Then what should I do with the mail?"

"Keep it. Unless there's something that looks very urgent; you can send that to this address; let me write it down."

Finally a letter came that looked urgent. I telephoned the address I'd been given. "There's a letter here," I said, "that looks urgent. Can you . . . should I send it on to you? Where is he?"

"I suppose," said a woman who didn't sound as if she thought it urgent at all. "I don't know where he is, honestly I don't."

"I don't mean to pry," I said.

"It's no secret," she said. "He's in Cuba."

Because I read mystery novels I began to wonder if my so-to-speak landlord was a genuine journalist, but when I looked up his name in a library, I found, to my disappointment, that every month or two he appeared in one magazine or another. He had been to Cuba before and had written three accounts of his visit, for *Maclean's*, the *Spectator*, and *Queen*. There were pieces on the theater in Prague, rural socialism in Yugoslavia, an academic dispute at the University of Toronto, and lots of reviews for English weeklies of books by Canadian writers. His style was distinguished for its impersonality, touched with a suggestion of "I would . . . if I could" and things unsaid but understood among friends: it was impossible to learn from his articles whether he was leftward or rightward in politics; whether he thought Canadian writing was comparable with contemporary stuff from France or America, or whether he thought it was a provincial disaster.

After reading his writings, I began to mention his name (these were the weeks of the boyfriend and the party), and everybody professed to know it, even to know him. "Oh, yes, Willie," was the typical response. "So that's where you're living, in Willie's flat."

One night I met a man who worked in a publishing house. Willie, he assured me, was in the American South, where he was writing about the civil rights movement.

A little more than three weeks after I had moved to Canon Square, I woke up late one morning and lay in bed, watching the sky for a bird or a change of hue upon the gray. Sometimes I dozed and the small noises of the house, pipes and drafts, filled my head so that I sank into sleep like a floating bottle that a wave tilts, and with a sigh is filled and sunk. And then I rose again. The clock said eleven, but it had stopped. I got out of bed and turned on the electric fire. I thought I heard footsteps.

"Who's there?" I said. "I'm coming."

The door of the flat opened upon a landing and a cascade of stairs, through darkness to the mat of light from the fanlight, three floors below. Walking downstairs, I saw that everybody's door was shut. In the mailbox there were two magazines for Willie Ferland and an advertising circular. I went upstairs again but hesitated on the threshold. "Is somebody there?" I said.

When there was no answer, I made myself go in and walk around the flat, from room to room. "Hello?" I said. "Hello, there?" Nobody was there.

Had there been somebody to ask me, "Do you think somebody got in the flat?" I would have said, No, I don't think so, because I did not think so in the ordinary way one thinks that, say, the telephone has rung or there's a strange noise from the garage. Rather it was as if a passing thought — "What if somebody darted into the flat while I went down for the mail?" — had lodged in my mind so tenaciously that it claimed a reality of its own and began to feed upon every sound and tilt of light. Or like a thought which, on the verge of sleep, becomes a dream.

I opened the closets. One held brooms and overshoes. Another held towels and a cigar box filled with prescription bottles. A third contained the immersion water heater and some stiff towels, left there to dry and forgotten. The closet in the bedroom was a big one with a rod at least six feet long. At one end hung my dresses and coats, with my suitcase open on the floor beneath them, spilling stockings, and at the other end of the rod were a few things that must have belonged to Willie: a green Irish sweater, a couple of jackets — one tweed and one corduroy — a Hudson's Bay wool shirt, and a dark blue woolen robe. I put on the robe and learned that Willie was a small man, for the robe almost fit me. In one pocket I found an expensive American ball-point pen, in the other a key on a piece of string. The warmth of the robe picked up my spirits; I went to the kitchen to make tea and then dialed the telephone to find out the time. It was almost three in the afternoon.

It began to rain. Straining over the sink, I could see the pavement round Canon Square darken, the only mother and child in the park hurry out of it, latching the iron gate behind them. I put Bach on the record player, ate toast with my tea, and chose one of Willie's books — he had stacks of them in the room that he used as a study, mostly Canadian novels. I read about a brave couple living alone in Saskatchewan. It grew dark. I switched on the lights and had sardines on toast for supper. The Bach record played over and over again until it began to sound comical, like a mechanical rainstorm. With Willie's ball-point pen I wrote a shopping list as an excuse to study my handwriting. It was nothing like Willie's. In the back of his books he had made notes for his reviews: his handwriting was small and upright, without ornament. I tried to copy it.

Willie Ferland, I wrote. My capitals were larger than his, my letters more florid.

Inaccuracies description p. 36 repeated later, I wrote, getting the knack of it: if I held the pen close to the tip, if I squeezed it tight and pressed each letter into the paper with a few hard strokes, I had the look of his writing. Yet only the look: the original was too small for me, done with an impulse of control I could not imitate. I essayed an independent sample:

> *Dear Mike: Sorry but my French isn't up to this. Who ever told you we were all bilingual? All my best, Willie.*

Comparing it with a paragraph penciled in the back of a guidebook to Quebec I thought my forgery looked convincing at first glance. But forgery didn't interest me; the spirit of the writing did. I found a sheet of paper in the drawer of his desk and wrote the word *description* several times; then I decided to look for more examples. The desk had two drawers, one with stationery and the other full of manila envelopes marked Yugo Co., Chichester etc., Anthlgy, and *Blue Over and Under*. Peeping inside the envelopes I found typescripts, and put them back.

The only other objects in the study, besides desk and chair and stacks of books without shelves, were two pasteboard boxes. I opened one and found it full of letters addressed to Willie, all of them put back into their torn envelopes; the other box was full of manila folders holding typewritten manuscripts. I could imagine what would happen if I were to go through the letters and the manuscripts and then turn to find that somebody had been watching me.

I turned, saying, "Yes?"

There was nobody there.

I lifted out one manila folder and closed the box. There were no curtains on the window in the study: from the window I saw the raincloud lit up by the sodium lights and dabs of light on the curtained back windows of houses behind Number 12. I made myself a drink from the single bottle of whiskey that Willie had left behind and wrote *Scotch, Teacher's* in his handwriting on the back of an envelope addressed to me.

The next morning Michael called me. "Who's this?" he asked when I answered the phone.

"It's me," I said.

"I thought it was someone else for a minute. So you're still there in your gloomy great flat, are you? Do you ever leave it?"

"Most of the time," I said.

"Would you leave it for an excursion to the cinema?"

"Yes," I said. "Anytime."

I dusted and threw out dead flowers and changed the sheets. I wore Willie's robe because it kept me warm, and I carried on imaginary conversations with Willie because they kept me occupied. *Have you been in this country long? I asked him.*

Ten years, he said. *Five years.*

You don't want me to know.

I'm secretive, he said. *Why do you want to know?*

Do you like it here? Will you stay?

What do you think?

I don't know, I said.

In the cabinet in the living room I found a set of highball glasses wrapped in store tissue, a windup tin train engine, ornamental matchboxes, a spring device for exercising the arms, and a half-dozen big enlarged photographs of a handsome woman with windblown dark hair. She looked everywhere but at the camera, she favored her right side.

Michael came and said, "Christ, this is dreary."

When we left Canon Square and got to a main thoroughfare, I was surprised to find that London was full of people. They hurried along the pavements with their heads down and umbrellas up; the women's boots smashed through the puddles; their shopping bags bumped and swayed. The butcher was almost hidden by a crowd of heads in scarves; his wife wrestled with the goods in the window, elbowing hanging sides of beef out of her way as she went for the tray of kidneys. We had to wait in line for our fish and chips; we were pushed against the wall as we ate. The pub was noisy and steamy; not an empty table in the lounge, the dart board busy. There was even a queue for the movie. We.bought chocolates and tickets for the middle stalls, and afterwards I said I'd had a super evening.

"Me too," Michael said.

We went to another pub, and in the closing-time uproar Michael said he was going to Bristol at the week's end: a job in social work had appeared; he didn't want to run the London office any longer.

"Why don't you come with me?" he said.

"Why?" I said.

"What's keeping you here?"

I was offended: "I have things to do."

"Oh, what?"

"I want to get a job teaching. I like London. I've been writing to the LCC — they might need somebody in the middle of the year. I expect I'll hear soon." It was a lie, but he had no reason to think so; instead he looked hurt and changed the subject.

The manuscript in the manila folder was a short story about a man who tries to get his wife into a lunatic asylum: he has taken a long train ride to the asylum so that he can talk to the doctors. They say that they have too many patients already, that they're understaffed. One doctor, a young Welshman, wants to talk only about what he could earn if he went into private practice. On the lawns of the asylum the patients take aimless walks or sit in the sun. An old man is lost and found again: the nurse comes to the psychiatrist's office to ask if he wants to see the old man. "Why shouldn't he try to escape?" the psychiatrist says. "It's the first sensible thing he's done. I don't want to see him." At last the visitor says he has to go back to London; the doctors advise him to care for his wife at home as long as he can manage it. The man leaves, and during the train ride back to the city, we learn he is not married.

"Who's there?" I said, when I finished it. I thought I'd heard a footstep. I called the number of the woman who thought Willie was in Cuba. To a housekeeper I said, "It's about Willie Ferland." Then a man came to the telephone.

"Willie," he said. "Is that you?"

I hung up without answering.

That evening the telephone rang, and a man said, "Hello, Willie? I heard you were back."

I didn't answer that time, but when the telephone rang again within a a minute I was scared he might call the police, and so I said, "Hello? Who is this?"

"Who's this? Is Willie there?"

"I'm afraid you have the wrong number."

"Is this EDGeware 4494?"

"This is EDGeware 3494."

"I'm sorry," he said.

He rang a couple of times but I didn't pick up the receiver. For the rest of the night, for the rest of the next day, I waited for the police, but nobody came. The telephone rang occasionally, but I would not answer it. Instead I went shopping for fresh flowers and Scotch, and I bought paper and envelopes — heavy, large cream sheets and large, stiff envelopes — to write to the London County Council.

"Dear Sirs," I wrote, "I am an American, just graduated from university, and having settled in London, I think I would like to teach.

"I have a B.A. degree in music and five credits of work in elementary education." But I hadn't. I had a B.A. in English and five or ten or fifteen credits in drama. I had signed for two courses in education and dropped them both; I could teach German expressionist drama, but that did not seem suit-

able for a London primary school. In the *New Statesman* I
read of appointments vacant: librarians, scientists, lecturers
in Anglo-African history at the University of Ibadan.

I twisted the heavy cream paper into spills and threw them
into the basket. On a fresh sheet of paper I wrote in Willie's
hand:

> *Dear Mike. No bloody luck with the jobs. I refuse
> to go to Malawi. Anything opening up at the magazine?
> Let me know soonest. Willie.*

The mail brought a book from Jonathan Cape, Ltd., a collection of Canadian verse. I skipped about in it and thought
it wasn't very good. On another piece of paper I composed a
note to Willie: "This came October 2 and I opened it because I was curious. I look forward to your review." As I
wrote I found myself trying to forge my own handwriting,
but the letters were too carefully drawn, and some of Willie's
mannerisms had crept in. So I copied the note again on the
typewriter and put it in the book.

The telephone rang. "Willie, listen." I'd never heard the
voice before. "I've got her in trouble, God help me. Do you
understand? Do you know a doctor?"

"Willie's not here just now," I said.

"Who is this?"

"I'm just visiting."

"Leave a message for him, will you? Tell him to call John
Webb. I don't suppose you know a doctor, do you?"

"No," I said. "Leave a number, and he'll call you."

"Tell him it's urgent."

"I will."

I called the fat man who worked for the BBC. "Listen,"
I said. "I'm sure you don't remember me, but I'm in an awful
fix. I'm pregnant, and I'm really stuck."

"I don't see what I can do," he said. "Sorry, darling."

"Listen, I have nobody else to ask."

"Wait a mo'."

The receiver smashed against something, and there were voices in the distance, a woman's voice sounding querulous.

"You *might* . . ." he said. "You might give this girl a ring. Explain everything to her. Be absolutely frank. Do you understand me?"

"Thank you, oh, I can't thank you enough," I said.

"That's all right," he said. "I'm sorry to hear it."

I called the number, and when a girl answered, I was absolutely frank: my boyfriend was an American airman in Germany, I said, and I'd got knocked up by this man in London, a married man, and my boyfriend was coming and I was desperate.

"Love, that's terrible," the girl said. She had a nice alert voice. "Love, I can't help you much, I can only give you the number of this doctor in Maida Vale. Ring him and see if he can help. Otherwise, I dunno. It's been a couple of years."

"You've been a great help," I said.

"If he's not there, ring me again," she said. "I'll ask my girlfriend."

Then I called John Webb. "Willie had to go out again," I said. "But he asked me to give you this number. It's a doctor in Maida Vale. He doesn't know if it's still any good or not."

"Kiss him for me, love," John Webb said.

That same day a woman called who said that she had just arrived from Vancouver and that she loved his articles, she had read every one.

"He'll be happy to hear that," I said. "I'm sorry he's not in just now."

"I'll be in London for the rest of the week."

"Try later," I said. "I just can't say when he'll be back.

But I'm glad you called. Lots of people don't realize that a writer doesn't get many compliments about his work. People think of writing to him and then they're shy. So I'll be sure to tell him you called."

"Thank you very much, Mrs. Ferland," she said.

I typed a note for Willie: *November 10, woman called to say she liked your articles, will call back."*

The telephone didn't ring again that day, and I didn't leave the house. Wearing Willie's bathrobe I lay on the couch in the living room, reading Canadian verse and listening to Mozart. The clock stopped again and the rain started again. When my stomach ached I convinced myself I hadn't recovered from appendicitis. I went to bed early and drew the curtains in the bedroom and fell asleep with the light on. Sometime, I don't know when, I sat up in bed with my heart pounding.

"Who is it?" I said. "Hello?"

The rain trickled against the window, and I didn't know if it was day or night: I got up and opened the closet and looked at Willie's jackets. They were so frightening: what if I had to get up and put on Willie's clothes? Was that what I had to do? Then why was I frightened? That meaningless fancy seemed peculiarly horrible to me: what if I had to get up and dress in his clothes and do what he had to do? There was a smell of self-hatred in the flat. He kept no mirrors, no photographs of himself, no souvenirs to remind himself of who he was. He put his letters back in their envelopes, ready to be returned. On some days no letters came at all. If he held his breath, he would disappear. But when I held my breath I could hear voices chattering on in my head, like a dozen radios from neighboring houses: "The bears. You will. Don't. Can in glory, here give Gladys. Exactly. That's exactly right. Do you have any of the other? Shelves. I can get it for you! Don't lie!" They were not real voices, I knew; they were words caught in my head, scooped up like lint as I had been this place and that place; then they settled on certain rhythms of my mind. Hearing but not listening I had collected these voices. Now I listened. A voice called my name.

"Who is it?" I said. Perhaps it had been a real one.

Nobody answered. I looked at the bedroom door and tried to get myself to open it, but I couldn't. I had to sit down on the bed, and then I had to lie down, and at last I fell asleep. Sometime later I woke up because the doorbell was ringing. I put on Willie's robe and went as quietly as I could through the apartment until I could hear their voices:

"Ella said he was back."

"Did you ring up?"

"No, but I expect he's here, that is, if he's here."

"I thought I heard someone inside."

"I don't hear anything. Push the bell again."

"Let's go."

"He might not want company."

Their footsteps dwindled away down the stairs.

That night I went to an Italian restaurant on the next block. I was the only customer. When the manager-waiter finished cutting ravioli on a table in the back of the room, he sat down with me.

"Very good food," I said.

"Where you from? I don't see you round this place."

"I live on Canon Square."

"No you don'. I never see you there. Where you live?"

"Number twelve."

"Then why don' I never see you? I live just across."

He went back into the kitchen. Now and then a passerby put his face to the window and stared at me.

"Business is slow," the manager said, when I paid him. "Winter comes now."

He turned the lights out when I left.

The streets were full of water: it soaked through the seams of my shoes and chilled my feet, soaked my stockings. In the lamplight I saw black spots on my legs where drops had flown up as I walked. The light was confusing: black shot with bright lights and reflections, cracks from drawn curtains, the oddly unilluminating brilliance of the streetlights. A taxi crashed past, only its parking lights on. When I got to the news agent's shop he was pulling down the shutter. "Wait," I said. "I'm closed, Miss," he said. "Sorry, I'm quarter of an hour late as it is. Sorry, Miss." So I went into a pub, where the drinkers stared as I entered the lounge. Then they started talking to each other again. A small table was free in the corner. "Whiskey, please," I said to the waiter; he brought whiskey and paper napkins and a dish of peanuts. I thought I heard somebody say "Whiskey" behind me, but when I turned my head, two middle-aged women were absorbed in a conversation. The sporting section of the *Telegraph* lay on the chair next to me, and so I read it and drank my whiskey and left. "Sorry," a man said, as we bumped at the door.

When I got to Canon Square I rang the doorbell, then ran up the stairs and knocked on the door. I found the key, unlocked the door. "Hello," I said. "It's me. I'm here." In the bedroom I took off my clothes and put on Willie's blue robe. In the living room I put on the Bach record and made myself a drink. "Yoo-hoo, it's just me," I said. I went to the closet with the towels and the box of pills and I studied each little bottle in turn. "Just looking," I said; then I remembered the story in the manila folder, and hurriedly I returned it to its place in the study.

"Yes?" I said. "Yes?"

A wind moved a door.

"I'm just in here," I said.

I thought of a voice saying, Why don't you like her? Well, she's, *you* know. I just don't. Don't ask me why. Who is she, after all?

Who's he?

"I'm in here," I said.

The telephone rang. "Is that you?" I said, and finally I picked it up. "Hello, who is this?"

"Who are you?"

"Who's this?" I said.

"Is Willie there?"

"Yes," I said. "Just a moment. Who shall I say is calling?"

"Tell him Joe Dolly."

"Can you hang on just a moment? Please?" I put the receiver gently on its side and walked from that room to the next and the next, calling, "Willie? Willie? It's Joe Dolly on the phone. Can you take it?" Then I went back to the phone and said to hold on, please.

"Willie?" I called. "Where are you? It's Joe Dolly."

"Oh, I'm awfully sorry," I said, at last. "He must have just stepped out. I don't know where. Down to the news agent's, I guess. Is there a number he can call back."

"Tomorrow'll do," he said. "Just remind him, would you? Tell him it's urgent."

"Right-o," I said.

By then I was convinced that he was coming back that night. I packed my suitcase, leaving only my raincoat on the rack, and I went over the bathroom looking for cosmetics and stray hairs. When the floor creaked, I said, "Yes? Hello?"

On the bed I laid out a wool dress and undergarments and a pair of jade earrings; then, out of curiosity, I picked up the clothes and threw them across the room. They hit the velvet curtains almost soundlessly and dropped to the floor. Next I drew a bath and got in but got out soon because the shapes under the water were strange, my legs looked too long, my back hurt. "I'm in the bathroom," I said, putting on Willie's robe again. "I'm almost ready."

The question was, where should I go? And so I waited in the living room, listening and looking for an answer; and after a while I learned I had to go to the bedroom. "I don't want to," I said out loud, but I went anyway; I opened the door and stepped into the room and closed the door again. There were six things in the room, as far as I could make out: the velvet curtains, the bed, a black night table, a lamp, a clock, and the closet. Some clothes lay on the floor in front of the curtain, so I put them out of sight on a shelf in the closet. After listening a while longer I learned I had to sit down on the bed. "I don't want to," I said again. I imagined Willie saying, *But I want to meet you. I'm sorry,* I said. Something wicked was going to speak to me, and I trembled, waiting for its voice. If you sat in the room as I did, and as he did, the voice would speak after a while, when it was quiet.

Then the voice began to speak. I didn't hear its words — that is to say, the words were as usual: confused, entangled in other words: "Interest of, now, let's, my goodness! here you hand me, she's going. Give it up. That's. An elephant, isn't it? You don't, careful, if you don't follow, how can you?" But I understood now.

"No," I said, as each temptation came to me in turn, as bright in my mind's eye as Christmas cards: the window over Canon Square — open, a fresh cold vowel of air spoken to me; then the shady gas oven; the pills — medicinal allsorts; and at last the razor blades — they were thin and new: a matter of brightness, colors galore.

"No," I said. "Please don't. Oh, please don't. I beg of you."

I hung onto the blankets; I caught the belt of Willie's robe and then pushed it away as if it were a snake, or a rope.

"Wait," I said. "Not yet."

Somebody called my name.

"Who's there?" I said. "Who said that?"

Nobody, nobody, nobody.

I ran out of the bedroom and opened the front door and looked down the stairwell; there was nothing to be seen, nothing to be heard. When I went back to the bedroom, I took off the robe and put on my wool dress and my coat and picked up my suitcase. I dialed the time: it was almost two in the morning. So I opened all the curtains, made a jug of coffee, and sat up the rest of the night in the living room with my suitcase at my feet. It was not until dawn that I could make myself write a note:

> Thank you for letting me use your flat. Everything is as I found it. I hope you had a good trip. Here is the key I was given.

A little after six in the morning I left the building and found a taxi and went to Victoria Station. The Southern commuter trains were already disgorging men with bowler hats and umbrellas; moving against their tide, I caught the first train to Paris, and from Paris I went on to Florence.

"Having a wonderful time," I wrote, in any old handwriting at all. It was a lie, anyway. The beautiful *things* pierced my heart like hatpins, but there wasn't a drop of blood left. I bought one notebook and then another to solicit the expression of my new-made heart, but there was nothing to say. From my reflection in the wardrobe's mirror I photographed my face and learned what *pinched* meant. My eyes were too pale. In the evenings, after going round the churches and museums, I ate enormous suppers and drank lots of wine. Nobody seemed to see me; the Italians did not notice me. In the mornings, with cappuccino, I ate up American papers, but I might as well have been the charlady's daughter. So one morning I threw away all my clothes. It was hard to do, but quick, like a painful inoculation. I took the dark dresses, the walking shoes and tweed skirts, and made a bundle of them and tied them with string and left them in a public lavatory. From my spy-hole across the street, the window of a pastry shop, I saw the toilet-paper lady go in, come out, the bundle in her hands. She turned it around and around, as if it were a bomb.

The salesgirls fell on me like pigeons on bread-crumbs. They had lipsticks that tasted like icing; their boyfriends had magical scissors, and my hair fell to the floor in a pale brown wreath around the barber chair. "I was robbed," I said in Italian, and to please them I added that the thief was a German tourist.

Sometimes, at night, I looked in the wardrobe mirror at the unfamiliar head and caught a *familiar* look, a knowing glance. "Are you there?" I asked. The girl in the mirror ran her tongue over her icing-pink lips and lifted her curls with her fingers: she was terrible, worse than anybody I could imagine. In the daytime she wore tight skirts and stockings that hissed as she walked. She took to smoking cigarettes, left ashes all over the table, left behind airmail editions of the London *Times*, but at last I decided she would not leave me, that nothing I could do would keep her away. She liked movies, after all, good food, strangers: at night, when I could feel the silence dissolve inside me like a pill in a glass of water, she got me out of the hotel, out to a café or a movie.

At Christmastime I went back to England. A girl I'd known at university had invited me to her house for Christmas, and she met me at Victoria.

"Gosh, look at you!" she said. Her look wasn't altogether happy. "Do you have any shopping to do before we go? I thought we'd take the six-forty train from Paddington."

"That's wonderful," I said. I began distributing money to porters, and my baskets and cases went into a taxi to Paddington; then from there I went in another taxi to Canon Square. A mean snowfall had left white streaks in the fenced park, and the lights were on in all the houses. At the top of Number 12 I seemed to see a light. The mailbox was empty, and I went up the stairs without ringing the bell downstairs. Only the bell beside the door. I could hear a new record on the Gramophone. Then it stopped. The door opened. Willie stood there in his blue bathrobe. His face was deathly white.

"I took care of the flat," I explained. "I wanted to thank you."

He looked me all over, but mildly, as if he didn't understand me. After a while he said, "Yes, you left a note. Do you want to come in?"

"I brought you something," I said.

It had not changed at all, except that there was a newspaper spread on the carpet in the front room and a tray of drinks on the record cabinet.

"This is it," I said. He opened the box and took out a bathrobe: it was white Italian wool, edged with cream-colored silk.

"This is a very expensive present," he said. "I thank you." Then he gave me a drink. "Who are you?" he said. "You're American, aren't you?"

"Yes," I said. "I'm American."

"You should lose your passport," he said, and laughed. Then he told me he had been in Quebec looking for a story about the Nationalists there. "I'm a Canuck," he said. "Didn't you know?"

"I thought of it," I said.

"I bet you did. But it's nothing. One wants to be something, but what is there to be? Now I wish I were an American, now that's something to be! Without a passport. Yes? Don't you feel it? It's worth traveling for, to *become* an American. Isn't that what's happened to you? How long have you been here? You were wrong to go to Italy, you should have stayed in London. Was everything all right here? What happened?"

"I just wanted to go to Italy," I said.

"Look at you," he said. "And this *present*. Do you understand what you've done?"

"What?" I said.

"I got the idea something had happened," he said.

"So did I," I said, and looked straight at him.

"Let me show you something," he said. He stood up and put his hands around my throat: they were as cold as glass.

"You'd better go," he said.

"Yes," I said. "I have to go. I have a lot to do."

"That's rich," he said. "Christ, you've become a crazy woman. You should try to control yourself." But he had the white bathrobe in his hands, and even as he spoke his hands explored the material; I could feel his interest fading like a breath on a cold window.

"You'll be back," he said.

But I never went back. That night Renata and I met at Paddington and got on the train stinking of perfume. We lighted cigarettes from my pack and drank gin from her picnic flask, and our laps and our coats were covered with fashion magazines. London disappeared into the dark; when we arrived at our destination, two boys were there to meet us. "Honey child," one of them said to me; and when he kissed me full on the mouth, I could taste fresh whiskey. "Who are you?" he said, after the kiss.